BTHE PLAINS

BLOOD ON THE PLAINS

TOM CURRY

WHEELER
CHIVERS

This Large Print edition is published by Wheeler Publishing, Waterville, Maine, USA and by BBC Audiobooks Ltd, Bath, England.
Wheeler Publishing, a part of Gale, Cengage Learning.
A Rio Kid Western Series.

Wheeler Publishing Large Print Western.
The text of this Large Print edition is unabridged.
Other aspects of the book may vary from the original edition.
Set in 16 pt. Plantin.
Printed on permanent paper.

LIBRARY OF CONGRESS CATALOGING-IN-PUBLICATION DATA

Curry, Tom, 1900–
    Blood on the plains / by Tom Curry.
      p. cm. — (A Rio Kid western series)
    ISBN-13: 978-1-59722-744-5 (pbk. : alk. paper)
    ISBN-10: 1-59722-744-7 (pbk. : alk. paper)
    1. Large type books. I. Title.
PS3505.U9725B56 2008
813'.52—dc22   2008003708

BRITISH LIBRARY CATALOGUING-IN-PUBLICATION DATA AVAILABLE

Published in 2008 in the U.S. by arrangement with Golden West Literary Agency.
Published in 2008 in the U.K. by arrangement with Golden West Literary Agency.

U.K. Hardcover: 978 1 405 64582 9 (Chivers Large Print)
U.K. Softcover: 978 1 405 64583 6 (Camden Large Print)

Printed in the United States of America
1 2 3 4 5 6 7 12 11 10 09 08

Blood on the Plains

CHAPTER I
HORSE-BUYER

Lieutenant Martin Grew, U.S.A., buying cavalry remounts for the Union forces, rode his dusty gelding through the gate into the H Bar yard.

"This is Haven's ranch, sir?" he asked of the big Kansan who got up from a bench shaded by the side of the house and came to him.

"Yes, Lieutenant. I'm George Haven."

Grew got down from his Army saddle. The chestnut wanted to get to the watering trough nearby. Haven watched as the officer, limping slightly, for he had been wounded at Gettysburg in the leg and was not yet fit for field duty, led his horse to water.

Grew was a tall, soldierly figure, his square shoulders shaping well into his blue tunic with its insignia. He wore a felt campaign hat strapped about his strong jaw. His blue trousers, with a wide yellow stripe at the seams, were tucked into his officer boots. At his side hung a saber.

He had pleasant dark eyes, and a crisp black mustache under a sharp nose. His face was heavily tanned, and thin, for he had lost weight during his suffering. Now he was temporarily assigned to the Quartermaster Corps until he was again ready for battle duty. He had a quick way of turning his head, and his long hands were restless, as he held the gelding's reins.

Haven helped him unsaddle and turned the chestnut into a nearby corral.

"Yuh look plumb wore out, Lieutenant," remarked the rancher. "And dry. How about a pitcher of cider?" He turned and sang out, "Oh, Edie! Fetch us some cider."

The rancher led the way over to the shaded bench, and they sat down, Grew mopping dust from his brow and features.

Haven was a man of middle age, with gray in his sun-faded hair. He had a broad face and clear blue eyes, a wide mouth that smiled easily. On his heavy body he wore a brown shirt and corduroy pants tucked into cowboots. His Stetson lay on the bench.

"I had your message, Haven," Grew said at once. "How many horses have you?"

"Eight hundred," replied Haven. "They ain't all mine, though. The folks round here, my neighbors, done rounded 'em up or bought 'em and we collected 'em at my ranch as it's nearest to town. Soon as yuh're rested, yuh can start lookin' 'em over. They're down behind the slope."

Grew had plenty of cash in the money-belts under his tunic. He had come to southeast Kansas on special detail, hunting horses for the military. The country had already been combed over in previous years and everything on hoofs had become scarce after the years of war.

Added to the demands of the Union Army, the C.S.A. had also been getting mounts out of Kansas in one way or another. Though Kansas was generally loyal, Missouri, next door, was with the South and burning hatred existed between the abolitionists and the slave state.

"I'm surprised," remarked Grew, "that Quantrell hasn't been through here."

Haven's lips tightened.

"Quantrell?" he growled. "Cuss him, he has. He come through last year and stole every danged head of hosses in sight! It near ruint us, I tell yuh. We scraped everything we had together to collect these animals we got here now and — well, if we mean to pull through, we got to make a good profit on 'em."

He fixed Grew's dark eyes, lines of anxiety in his brow.

"The U.S. Government will pay well for good animals," assured Grew.

There was a light step behind him and he looked around, in that quick way of his. His glance had been casual, but his eyes widened alertly as they took in the girl who had come from the kitchen lean-to, carrying a tray on which reposed a pitcher of golden cider, a plate of home-made doughnuts, and two glasses.

Grew jumped to his feet, to bow. In her clean gingham dress she was a most attractive girl. The ever-present wind of the Kansas plains whipped at her light curly hair. Long lashes veiled her violet eyes, her lips were full and red — all her features approaching perfection. She was a small girl, and perhaps seventeen or eighteen years old. Her young figure, while showing approaching maturity, had a frailty that was appealing.

She started to set the tray on the bench but Lieutenant Grew took it from her hands before she could stoop. She flashed him a quick smile, the color deepening in her smooth cheeks.

"My daughter Edith," said Haven, his attention on the refreshments. "Help yoreself,

Lieutenant."

"Thank you, Miss Haven," Grew said softly.

His eyes were frankly admiring and she was impressed by this tall man who seemed to be a melancholy figure. In his face was a brooding look, a sadness brought by the War and the anguish through which he had gone.

"We have fried chicken for supper, Lieutenant," Edith said, her words an invitation.

"Oh, shore," Haven agreed. "He savvies he's welcome, don't you, Lieutenant? Nothin' shy about the Army." The rancher laughed as he poured the cider and pushed the doughnuts toward Grew. "Have some fried holes. They're mighty good the way Edie makes 'em. It'll take you a day or two to check them horses, so yuh might as well make yoreself to home."

"Thanks." The officer nodded. "It will be a great pleasure."

Edith Haven smiled again, nodded, and went back toward the kitchen. Grew watched her girlish figure until she had turned the corner, then he set about refreshing himself. He was thirsty and the cider was cool and just hit the spot.

"Where's yore home, Lieutenant?" inquired Haven, his mouth full of doughnut.

"I come from Kansas."

"Oh, you do, huh? Not these parts?"

"A hundred miles north, on the Kaw. At least, it was there when I left for the Army."

"Yuh don't say! Yuh're mighty young. Yore folks livin'?"

A spasm of pain flitted across Grew's face. He shook his head. It was hard for him to think about it, let alone discuss it.

Haven was a friendly man, though. He didn't mean to hurt Grew, but kept on asking about his home and people. Finally Grew had to explain.

"Quantrell and his men burned our home," he said grimly. "My Father was shot and killed during the raid, and my Mother died soon after from shock."

"I shore am sorry!" mumbled Haven. He blinked, realizing he had put his foot in it. "Have another doughnut, Lieutenant. Dang the dust! It's in everything. We'll have a storm tonight."

The sun was dropping to the edge of that vast prairie ocean, the plains of Kansas that were covered with short, curling grass. Along the streams were belts of timber, cottonwoods and scrub oak, but the undulating rises were like some tremendous sered sea paralyzed there to immobility by a magic hand. Haze was in the sky, dust hung thick and there was the threat of the imminent storm of which Haven had spoken.

The house was of sod bricks and unseasoned timber, which had dried and cracked in the sun. There was a sod barn, and fences of rails and wire. Here Edith kept house for her father, for Haven, a widower, had lost his wife a decade before.

Nearby ran a creek, a tributary of the Verdigris River. Cottonwoods and other growth bordered the waterway, and around the bend where the ranch was built were the horses, hidden from the house by the trees.

Haven led Grew over there. The animals were grazing in bunches, in a great corral, and several men were guarding them, friends of Haven's.

"Night shift's sleepin' in the timber," informed Haven. "But supper'll soon be ready, Lieutenant. In the mornin' yuh can start goin' over these hosses."

Oddly, though, as Lieutenant Grew talked to Haven, and as interested as he was in the horses, his thoughts were more for Edith. Edith Haven, he thought, must be a busy young woman.

And she was. She had to cook for all the herders, gathered here now to care for the horses. And the odors of the food she was preparing were appetizing.

Grew cleaned up thoroughly, brushing off as much dust as he could from his uniform. He washed and shaved with the razor he carried in his Army kit. When he had finished, the sun was red and apparently enlarged as it touched the horizon of the plains. The haze was like smoke from a prairie fire in the burnished sky.

Ready for supper, he went inside with George Haven.

The house was furnished with crude chairs, tables, and bunks. Small windows let in slits of light but as darkness fell the candles and the lamp that were lit made it cozy.

Edith rang a brass-tongued bell, and cowmen came riding in answer to it. They were one shift of the guard watching the valuable horses below. Grew was introduced to them by the hearty Haven.

"This is Milt Young — owns the Star Two next my ranch," Haven said. "He's got three sons with Gen'ral Grant."

Young, a stocky, heavy man, with a strong, bearded chin, good features and determined brown eyes nodded to the lieutenant, smiling greetings. Then others were introduced.

Grew tried to memorize the names of the Kansans as he met them. He had a methodical mind and readily placed them all. There were the Phillips brothers, Jake and Ben, great, breezy raw-boned cowmen with red skins. They had come up from Texas to settle on the plains.

They were in their early forties, and each had his son along now, young fellows of sixteen who had not yet entered the Army. Then there was "Pop" Schultz, a bewhiskered rancher whose spread was to the west of the Star 2.

Most young men were at war and the fathers were holding the range and doing the work while they were gone. But there was one young man, Fred Olliphant, about Grew's age, who had been discharged from the Army because of crippling wounds.

They were all friends and neighbors of Haven's, good citizens and hard workers. They wore riding clothes, heavy boots with spurs, leathered pants, sweated shirts and wide hats. All were experts with cattle and horses, and they had put all they had into the horses collected here now to be sold.

After greeting Grew, they took their places at the long board table in the lean-to and Edith set the plates of food on the table. There were pots of coffee to wash it down.

As they began to wolf the meal, someone rode up to the front, and George Haven got up and went to see who called.

"Why, howdy, Thompson!" Grew heard him sing out. "Light and eat. C'mon in."

Grew glanced around. A huge man entered, stooping to get through the doorway. He wore the blue of the Union Army and his insignia told that he was a major. Grew arose and saluted.

"Sit down, Lieutenant, sit down," Major Thompson cried. "Never mind formality here."

The man was tremendous, with a hogshead chest bulging out his dusty tunic, and a great head of crisp curly, iron-gray hair. He had thick lips and his weather-lined cheeks were decorated with "Burnside" whiskers.

"He must tip the scales at two-fifty!" thought Grew, astonished at the physical might of Thompson. The major was one of the largest men he had ever seen.

"Lieutenant Grew, this here is Major Jarvis Thompson," George Haven introduced. "Pull up a chair, Major. There's plenty to eat."

Thompson smiled and bowed. He was quick to mirth as attested by myriad wrinkles about his deep-set blue eyes, and he was hearty, bluff. His hairy hands were like hams. Obviously he was as strong as a bull, which animal he resembled, and the chair creaked under his weight as he sat down at the other side of his host.

"I've been on a special mission," Thompson told Haven, "and have to be in Lawrence by midnight. However, I'll enjoy a bite. Lieutenant, I suppose yuh're on special detail out here?" His eyes were keen as they fixed Grew.

"Yes, sir. For the Quartermaster General."

"He's come to look over them hosses, Major," explained Haven. "You seen some of 'em when yuh passed by last week. We figger on sellin' 'em to the Army."

Thompson nodded. "If the ones I saw were samples, the cavalry's in for luck. . . . Mighty dry today, wasn't it?"

"Yeah, but it's goin' to storm tonight."

The talk went on in that desultory fashion, and after the first shift had eaten, the men went to relieve their friends. Grew met more of the local ranchers, men of the same fine type as their friends when the second shift came in to eat.

The wind was picking up speed and whistling more shrilly as it fought at the corners of the house. Dust was flung against the rough panes and the whole world seemed to hum. The night grew darker, the stars and moon obscured by the storm. Suddenly what sounded like a shower of stones

17

pattered on the roof.

"Hail!" exclaimed Haven. "Major, yuh'll have a mean ride tonight."

Thompson grinned. "I'd better start. I reckon my hoss can make it though. He has to be strong to carry me in the first place."

He threw his cheroot butt into the blazing fire in the stone fireplace and heaved up his great bulk.

All the cowmen had gone back now to guard their precious horses, and Haven had some leather work to do, mending a broken bridle and saddle strap. Thompson pulled his black cloak about his heavy body. He shook hands with Grew and Haven, saluted Edith politely, and went out into the dark.

Grew went over into the lean-to, as Haven busied himself with his work.

"May I help you?" he asked the girl, who was cleaning up after the meal.

"Thank you." She smiled at him. "But don't if you're tired."

"I'm not," he said, and smiled back. "It will be a pleasure."

He took the dish towel and dried the tin plates and mugs for her. And it was a pleasure to him to enjoy such domesticity, even if only for a short time.

CHAPTER II
GUERRILLAS

Since such folk must rise at daybreak, they turned in early. Haven was yawning mightily by nine o'clock.

Edith said good night and retired to her small room off the kitchen. Grew was to sleep in the bunk across the main room where Haven slept.

The storm was shrieking wildly outside, deafeningly as the two men prepared for bed. Suddenly there was a sharp, snapping noise. Grew, who had just bent to pull off his boots, thought it was a breaking stick of wood, but as he glanced over he saw Haven doubling up on the floor with a stricken look on his face, his eyes wide, glazing. Blood was on his left cheek.

At that moment, as he jumped, something burned along his ear, stinging frightfully, and plugged into the wall back of him.

Only one candle was still burning, and Grew, realizing that someone was shooting in through the narrow window opposite, threw a boot at the light, ducking to seize his Colt Army pistol. The boot hit the candle and knocked it out, plunging the room into darkness.

More were shooting in, but it was blind shooting now. Grew was cool under fire and watched the streaking flashes of the revolvers hunting him, crouched out of the line of the slugs at one end of his bunk. He took aim at a flash and pulled trigger. His heavy revolver kicked back against his hand, and he heard a cursing shriek from an attacker outside.

It was all confusion, dark confusion. Grew had no idea who was attacking, or why. His first thought, though, was of the girl, and he edged toward her room, after delivering another shot that tore too close for comfort to the killers at the window.

They slackened their fire, but more of them began whooping it up outside the door. The lieutenant reached out and dropped the bar-bolt.

In his bare feet, Grew glided swiftly toward Edith's room. Suddenly he bumped into someone moving.

"Father — Father! What is it? Are you hurt?"

It was Edith. She threw her arms around

Grew's neck and clung to him tightly.

"It's Lieutenant Grew," he whispered. He held her, but she realized the mistake she had made in the darkness, and drew away.

"Is my father there?" she asked anxiously.

"He's hit — wounded. Take it easy. We've got to —"

"I smell smoke."

The attackers had been banging on the front door. Now Grew also caught the odor of burning hay. Some had been brought over and piled against the door, and smoke was blowing in through the smashed windows. Already a faint ruby glow, whipped by the high wind, showed in the night.

"We must get your father out, and quick," Grew told Edith. "Can you handle a gun?"

"I can shoot a pistol."

"Good. Take mine, then. I'll pick up your father's. There's a back door, isn't there?"

"Yes. I keep it locked at night."

"It's still dark at the rear. We can make the screen of brush along the creek if we're lucky. You stand by to open the door, and I'll fetch your father. Hurry, now!"

"But our men will come up to help us, I'm sure —"

Grew shook his head.

"We mustn't count on that. We must escape while we have the faintest chance."

21

She did not argue. Grew ran back and, by feeling near the bunk, found the unconscious rancher. Haven had not budged since he had gone down. He was still alive, although Grew felt the warm, sticky blood as he touched Haven. He located Haven's Colt, a Frontier Model .45, and threw several bullets out one of the front windows. They drew howls and slugs from the attackers.

Giving them this to think about, Grew leaped back to Haven, picked the rancher up, and hurried to the lean-to. Edith waited for him, pistol in hand. She unbolted the door, and Grew started out, holding Haven over his shoulder with his left hand, his right free to use the gun.

"Hey — hey! Here they come!"

Grew saw a dark figure at the corner of the house, against the mounting red glow. He snapped a shot that way and had the pleasure of making a hit, the fellow folding up in his tracks at his post.

But his subterfuge inside had drawn the rest to the front, and the wind, away from the deafened ears of the raiders, carried off even the heavy explosion of the Colt.

Edith led the way, with Grew at her heels. The wound he had taken was superficial and in the tense excitement he did not remember about it at all. Two hundred yards away lay the comparative safety of the brush along the creek, and within a couple of minutes they were plunging into the thickets, behind them the fired house.

The wind shoved the flames at all that was combustible, and Grew, looking back, saw wild figures dancing about in the redness. There were half a dozen there that he could count.

The escaping trio were gasping for breath. But the girl's chief concern was for her father, and Grew placed Haven as comfortably as possible under the circumstances.

He tore a piece of his shirt off and wadded it.

"Hold this to the bleeding," he whispered. "Don't strike any light or make any noise. I'm going to reconnoiter."

Suspicion was in his shrewd mind. The wind was sweeping into the thickets, rattling seed pods and leaves, and the shriek of it made the ears ring. But as Grew moved down around the bend, he began to hear heavy shooting. It came from the spot where the horses had been held.

However, as he worked his way through the brakes, he realized that the animals were gone, either driven off by the raiders or else stampeded by the battle. A flash of lightning showed the big open space, the corral where they had been held.

Several mounted men, shooting into the brush farther upstream, evidently had someone treed there, for Grew saw the reply as the Colts barked, and concluded it was one of Haven's friends who had been with the horses.

In the lightning flare, the quick panoramic view did not give him many details, although he saw a writhing horse on its back, and two or three dead men on the field. Then the night and the wind closed in.

He would have liked nothing better than to open fire on the moving, shadowy assassins, but he could not bring them down on Edith and her wounded father. Then he saw them moving off, back toward the burning house.

He heard gunfire across the creek then, and turned that way, squatting in the dense bush on the bank.

The thunder of thousands of hoofs for a few minutes drowned out the roar of the storm. Big bunches of mustangs dashed by. He could see them vaguely against the sky, and another lightning play showed hard-riding men shoving the animals along. There were, he estimated, fifty or sixty of the human centaurs, shooting and yelling.

But then they were gone, and he turned, going back to the spot where he had left Edith.

She was crouched there, tending her father. Up the slight slope, the wooden parts of their home burned fiercely in the wind, but the raiders who had attacked the house had gone.

"They rode off southeast," the girl told Grew.

The rancher had stopped bleeding, the officer was relieved to find. Haven was grunting and swearing under his breath, coming back to consciousness. There was a bad crease across his scalp on the left side, the bullet having missed killing him only by a fraction of an inch. It had torn a gash in his cheek and knocked out two teeth, which had somewhat deflected it and caused it to miss Haven's chin.

"They've taken your horses," Grew informed the girl gravely. "No doubt that's what they were after. There were sixty or seventy of them, at least."

"I — I hope they didn't kill our friends."

She kept good control of herself, thought Grew, with deep admiration. Pioneer women like Edith had a great deal to face, and she had their resolute, calm courage.

The barn had not been fired so, after making sure that the raiders had gone, Grew carried Haven to that building. All horses, including Grew's own Army mount, had been run off.

Within shelter, Grew and Edith watched her home burning, saw the roof cave in, all that was built of wood consumed. After an hour, when Haven had revived but was still weak from shock, several riders approached, carefully. Grew recognized them as some of the ranchers, the cowmen who had been guarding the horses that had been stolen.

Milt Young, with a bullet tear in his left forearm, and riding a wounded horse, led them. Jake Phillips was supporting his brother Ben, who had a nasty injury in one hip where a .45 slug had nicked the bone. Pop Schultz had been thrown to the plain when his mustang had been shot from under him, and one cheek was a bloody mess.

All those men had felt the enemy lead that night, and back on the field of battle lay two dead men, Fred Olliphant and Sam Green. Others who had been beaten back, pursued and gunned despite their stout defense, were not yet in.

When the ranchers came up to the barn they explained that while they had been held by some raiders, others of the crew had driven off the horses.

"That sorta finishes us, boys," growled Milt Young, as he washed his wound in the trough near the barn. "Quantrell's got him some fine hosses. I hate to go home and tell the old lady what's happened. We needed the money them hosses would bring."

The others told the same story. They had banked everything on the band of mustangs they had with such difficulty got together to sell the Army.

"You're sure it was Quantrell's gang?" growled Lieutenant Grew, voice thick with baffled fury.

"No doubt at all," replied Milt. "I seen that devil Cole Younger. And I'm shore I reckernized Todd — he's Quantrell's murderin'est lieutenant, if yuh pick one from the other in that bunch of cutthroats. Cuss 'em."

"I seen Quantrell hisself," chimed in Jake Phillips. "He's the one who shot pore Ben . . . Give me a hand, gents. We got to probe for this bullet. Somebody hold him down."

Quantrell! Kansas shuddered at the name. Sweeping in with his guerrilla raiders, showing no mercy, burning and pillaging under the pretense that it was warfare and that he was commissioned by the Confederacy for such devil's work, Quantrell was a night-mare to the citizens of Kansas. The C.S.A. appalled by his methods, had finally repudi-ated him.

He was actually outlawed now by both sides of the warring forces.

Martin Grew had just cause to loathe Wil-liam Quantrell, who had killed his father and was responsible for the sudden death of his mother. Now again he saw the awful suf-fering caused by the guerrillas. Edith, who already had touched his heart, was shocked and homeless and her father had been seri-ously hurt.

Decent men had died here tonight, trying to guard their rightful property.

It meant sorrow and mourning for other homes throughout the district, to say noth-ing of the financial ruin wrought.

"Somebody's got to capture Quantrell and his gang!" Grew muttered grimly.

Chapter III
Military Mission

Captain Robert Pryor, U.S.A., had been summoned by an aide to report at the quarters of his brigade commander, General George A. Custer, the brilliant star of the Union Cavalry. Pryor walked rapidly across the company street to the tent where the general's guidon flew from its staff.

There was tremendous, leashed power in his springy stride. In the first flush of young manhood, Pryor was a glowing example of American strength, the type of fighting man who had sprung to the colors when the country had called.

He wore the Union blue and was a striking soldierly figure in his neat tunic with the brass buttons shined and gleaming, his speckless riding boots, with the silver spurs shining in the sunlight. Down the seams of his pants ran the wide yellow stripe showing the cavalry was his branch of service, and a captain's insignia placed his rank. He wore a felt campaign hat, with a taut strap around his determined chin, and was fresh-shaven, clean.

There was a rosy glow to Captain Pryor's tanned cheeks, for he hailed from Texas, near the Mexican border. Down there his nickname had been "The Rio Kid." From boyhood he had ridden dangerous frontier trails, punching cattle, breaking horses, fighting Indians and raiders. From the time he could hold a rifle and Colt he had been trained with firearms, and was an expert shot with both. Born to the saddle and the life of a pioneer, Pryor had proved invaluable as a scout and aide to Custer. Pryor had long since grown used to peril and thought nothing of it.

He was broad-shouldered and tapered to a narrow waist, where rode his saber and Army pistols. His chestnut hair was close-cropped, his features pleasant although in his quick blue eyes there was a reckless, devil-may-care light. One look at him was reassuring, for plainly here was an efficient man, one who was afraid of nothing. He was a man who could command men, but he could also do a good job traveling alone.

The sentry at Custer's tent presented arms, and announced him. The general's clear young voice called to him to enter.

Pryor went in, came to attention and saluted.

Custer returned the salute, then nodded and waved toward a canvas chair.

"Sit down, Captain Pryor."

The Rio Kid worshiped his commander. All Custer's men loved him. He was the best fighting cavalryman in the Army. He could go to the inferno and back — and they would follow.

At twenty-three he was a brigadier, and it was rumored that before long he would wear two stars on his shoulders. For Sheridan put full trust in Custer.

Besides being a fine soldier, Custer was also a handsome man, striking, with his tawny mane and flowing mustache. He had a flair for fancy uniforms and equipment which all the young officers envied and tried to emulate — his only real vanity.

"You're going on a special mission, Captain," Custer said, without preliminary.

His fine eyes were on Pryor. He noted the anxiety that came into the Rio Kid's eyes, and smiling, he added: "You won't miss much fighting here in the next month, Captain. I can promise you that. The brigade's been ordered back to quarters for refurbishing and rest. You'll see a lot more action than we will."

"Thank you, General."

"Come along, then. I'll ride to Headquarters with you."

A few minutes later, the Rio Kid, mounted on his warhorse, Saber, rode alongside the dashing Custer, who was mounted on a great black charger.

Saber, a mouse-colored dun, had a black stripe down his spine, a mark that was believed to belong only to "the breed that never dies." While not prepossessing in looks, the horse could run faster than any Pryor had ever met up with. He had a bad temper with other horses and with everybody save his master who had brought him up from a colt.

One big eye was mirled with blue and white streaks and it rolled wickedly now as he measured the distance between the black and his teeth. Saber enjoyed fighting with other horses, as he actually enjoyed men's battles. He would gallop toward the sound of guns if not restrained, and was fully trained to give his rider all the advantages in a hand-to-hand combat.

General Custer rode with Captain Pryor the three miles to GHQ. Dismounting, and handing over their horses to orderlies, they approached the quarters of the general in command of the Union forces.

Entering the big tent, they approached the man slouched in a camp chair, his bearded chin sunk on his breast. His tunic was partially unbuttoned and cigar ashes clung to the blue cloth. He gripped a half-smoked West Indian cheroot between his teeth. He was hatless, his boots were muddy and run over at the heel but there was authority in every line of this man, this General Grant, as he turned his narrowed blue eyes on the two debonair cavalrymen.

A faint twinkle came across his vision, as he carelessly acknowledged their bandbox salute.

"Gentlemen," he drawled, "you are punctual to the second."

He waved his hand and the generals and other high officers of Headquarters Staff who were with him left the tent. Only Captain Pryor, General Custer and another young captain of cavalry remained with Grant.

General Ulysses S. Grant had proved himself a soldier on the Mississippi. He had won those campaigns, and President Abraham Lincoln, frantically searching for a commander who could win battles instead of talking about tactics, had placed him in charge in the East.

The stocky Grant, despite his sloppy dress

and careless personal mannerisms, was the Man of the Hour. And only a few short years before, at the beginning of the Civil War, Grant had been a failure, a clerk in his father's store in the Middle West. He had risen to the heights with meteoric speed.

"You know Captain Edward Terrell of the Fourth Kansas?" Grant said, waving toward the stalwart, mustached young officer at his other side.

Custer and Pryor greeted Terrell. They were acquainted with him, knowing him as a fine cavalryman and efficient officer. He wore the same type of dress as did the Rio Kid, but he was a man larger in build than the Kid. He had darkish hair.

"I asked you for your best scout, General," Grant said to Custer, with an inquiring glance at Bob Pryor.

"And, sir," Custer replied, "I have brought him. This is he — Captain Robert Pryor."

"This is a special mission," Grant said at once, without formality. "Captain Terrell's home is in south Kansas and he lived in northern Missouri as a boy. You are to work together, but Terrell will have charge of the uniformed forces. Your mission, Pryor, is to work in the field, as you see fit, and if possible supply Terrell with information leading to the arrest of the enemy we are after. That enemy, in short, is William Clarke Quantrell. You've heard of him?"

Grant was looking hard at the Rio Kid.

"Yes, General," the Kid replied. "The guerrilla chief."

"That's the man. He operates chiefly against Kansas, out of Missouri. For a time he was attached to the Confederates as an irregular, but they have repudiated him because of his blood-thirsty methods. Captain Terrell is personally acquainted with Quantrell, which is why he has been chosen to lead the expedition.

"The object is the arrest of Quantrell and the destruction of his band. Their raids have grown to major proportions and his force constitutes a menace to our supply and to loyal citizens in Kansas and nearby states.

"I have here, besides many complaints from the citizenry and various Congressmen who represent them, a report sent in by Lieutenant Martin Grew of the QMC. While he was negotiating for the purchase of several hundred horses for the Army, Quantrell attacked and ran them off. This is only one of Quantrell's exploits. He must be checked."

Grant nodded. The interview was over. Written orders were handed the two captains, and Terrell and Pryor took their leave. . . .

More than a week later, Captain Bob Pryor, still wearing his uniform instead of the scout outfit he affected for such purposes, rode across the dusty, flat Kansas plain toward the town of Lawrence.

Captain Terrell had left him, going to take charge of the Union detachment. Now the Rio Kid, who was on special Intelligence, was pressing on toward the heart of the country that seemed to be at the mercy of Quantrell and his guerrillas. Pryor meant to talk with Lieutenant Martin Grew, whose report he had read, and with the ranchers who knew Quantrell, to their sorrow. He wanted to get a first-hand idea of where the elusive guerrilla chief might be hiding.

He had risen at daybreak from his bivouac, had spruced up, cared for the dun, Saber, and hurried along.

The sun was just coming up when he heard sudden, heavy gunfire ahead. Dust rolled high into the blue sky and smoke began to roll up from the buildings of Lawrence as he galloped toward the town.

The fields were green, and birds chirped in the trees, but ahead there seemed to be chaos in the small city which had, shortly before, been at peace. To approach, Pryor still had to cross the Kansas River, and on his side of the stream was a small camp of militia. The soldiers there, surprised by the sudden attack on the settlement, were milling about, shouting, some shooting across the river. A line of men over there fired into them, holding them at bay.

Saber snorted, veering toward the guns. Pryor whipped him along. Finding a crossing, he pushed into the water, upstream from the direct line of fire.

Shrieks, gunshots, the banging of pistols and rifles, all in all a pandemonium had seized upon Lawrence. Through the streets rode madmen, killing, putting the buildings to the torch. Already smoke was rolling high into the air.

Not knowing as yet what was up, the Rio Kid, with his Colt drawn, drove in on the confused scene. He guessed that the enemy had attacked, but could not tell what forces were engaged. It seemed impossible that such a large town, garrisoned with troops, could be raided by guerrilla fighters, but there was apparently no organized resistance.

On a dirt road, he flashed past the smoldering ruins of a small Army camp. Dead men lay all about — young fellows, most in their 'teens, cadets who had been wiped out by the first charge of the enemy.

In the center of the town a woman stood on a street corner, her eyes wide, her face tortured with the utmost horror. Both hands were held to her burning cheeks, and she was screaming wildly:

"My son — my husband! They're dead! Quantrell — Quantrell! Murder!"

She was only one among hundreds. Butchery was proceeding with mass speed. Through the town the guerrillas, powerful men, some in stolen Union blue or in Confederate gray, or in nondescript clothing, were methodically killing. They used Colt revolvers chiefly, dashing up to fire point-blank into any who dared show resistance. Others were looting homes and stores, and setting the torch to dry buildings.

The walks and dirt roads were filled with dead, and with writhing wounded.

The wind swept the smoke through the settlement, obscuring the vision. Dry wood crackled as it roared into flame. Many had leaped on their horses and run for it, or taken to the woods along the river.

Pressing in, identifying the enemy by their appearance and actions, the Rio Kid sought to help the luckless people of Lawrence. But as his uniform was seen, a band of a dozen guerrillas set up a howl and turned their horses toward him. He let go with his Colts, and one crashed dead from his horse. But the others came on, driving crazily at him.

There were more on his flanks. He was outnumbered. There were hundreds of the killers in the settlement, and he was driven back, with bulletholes in his clothing and hat, and with scratches from close shots that had torn his flesh.

With fighting fury, the Rio Kid was shoved to the outskirts of town. The guerrillas tried to ride him down but the dun was too swift even for the picked, fast-running animals mounted by Quantrell's gang.

For the moment, at least, his defeat was complete.

CHAPTER IV
DEATH AND
DESTRUCTION

Wanton destruction and carnage in Lawrence made the town a scene of horror. Here, as in other places, there was little organized resistance as yet to Quantrell's bloody, bold attack, and wherever any started it was promptly crushed by the guerrillas.

Murder stalked the streets of Lawrence and the choking black smoke from burning buildings rolled through the warm air, making it difficult to see what was happening. Screams, the roar of a thousand guns and of leaping flames sounded in the ears of terrified citizens who could not believe their senses. What was occurring was a nightmare, but they were forced to believe, for Quantrell showed no mercy and his followers killed without the slightest compunction, for the sport of it, then seized any loot they fancied.

The knot of guerrillas tearing on the Rio

Kid's trail kept coming like determined wolves. One mounted on a long-limbed, beautiful bay gelding, spurted out ahead of the others, gradually drawing closer to Bob Pryor, who purposely slowed the dun.

Quantrell's man had two Colts in his hands. His reins were in his bared teeth for the purpose, and a snarl of rage and hate was in his throat. He was a huge fellow, with tow hair flying in the wind, because his hat was off and hanging behind him by the leather strap.

The stolen Union blue tunic he wore was dirty and unbuttoned. His corduroy pants were torn, his black boots filthy. But despite the slovenly appearance of this unshaven man with his fishy, bloodshot eyes and his nostrils flared with killer excitement, he was a most dangerous opponent, a typical guerrilla, ready to kill without the slightest excuse. A looter, but a hard-riding, dead-shooting devil.

Knee pressure swerved Saber slightly and the guerrilla, who had held his fire until he was almost on the Rio Kid, missed with both guns because of Pryor's sudden maneuver, though only by inches. The Rio Kid had swung the dun around in the charging killer's path.

He had a swift impression of blazing eyes,

of teeth with the reins clenched between them, as the man loomed upon him. Then, with Saber steadying for a breath under his signal, Pryor let go.

The guerrilla was coming too fast to swerve enough. He took the Rio Kid's lead in the nose. The slug smashed through his brain and he flew off the bay, dead before he folded in the dust. The horse dashed on past Pryor.

A concerted howl of fury rose from bearded throats as the hard-riding rascals on Pryor's trail saw him triumph over their comrade. They dug their spurs deep, making a maddened charge straight onto his blasting pistols, determined to tear him to bits with their bullets. He threw lead into them but they spread out to draw him into a net and he was forced into retreat again.

One man against an army, cut off from the Kansas River now by the foe, and with the infantry in camp over there paralyzed by the deadly fire from the guerrillas watching them! The Rio Kid realized this as he rode away, his guns snarling back at his enemies.

They pressed him hard, deadly shots every one, and he had to let the dun show his best speed in order to escape. That bay, riderless, ran on before Saber, tail and mane flying, snorting. He had a slight wound on his flank and was crazy with the excitement. With no weight to carry, he kept galloping fast.

The determined guerrilla bunch stayed on the Rio Kid's trail for miles, howling and cursing, trying to pick him off with long shots. But as the smoke pall over Lawrence grew distant and the awful sounds in the town died away, they slowed, glancing back. Apparently they were growing anxious about being cut off in case their companions should be driven out of Lawrence by mounting resistance and the arrival of reinforcements from nearby Federal troop encampments.

Topping one of the regular wavelike rises in the prairie ocean, the Rio Kid saw dust ahead. Riders were coming his way. He veered off, not knowing whether they might be enemies or friends.

At sight of this, the guerrillas also stopped. A man on a white horse, his dark blue uniform showing plainly against the animal's flanks, and trailed by a dozen riders in cowboy garb, set up a shout as he saw the wolfish fellows chasing the Rio Kid.

One of the cowmen took the coiled lariat from its hook by his saddlehorn and spurred after the riderless bay. The rope loop whistled out, settling over the running horse's head, and the bay came to a halt.

Quantrell's men fired a volley, which was answered by the uniformed man on the white horse, and his cowboy companions. Then the guerrillas turned their horses and went galloping back to Lawrence to rejoin their band.

The Rio Kid carefully approached the riders ahead of him. They had pulled up and were staring at the smoke pall hanging over Lawrence.

"Hi, there!" sang out Pryor, raising a hand in the universal signal of friendship common to the Frontier. "Who are you?"

"I am Lieutenant Martin Grew," called the tall young man on the white horse. "U.S.A."

"I'm in luck," thought the Rio Kid. Grant had mentioned Lieutenant Grew, who had written a report on previous raids made on Kansas by Quantrell. He had intended to contact Grew, and here was his man on the spot.

The cowboy who had roped the bay from whose back Pryor had shot Quantrell's man, came slowly in, leading the captive horse, and joined his companions. They eyed the Rio Kid as he slowly rode over to them. They had seen the guerrillas pursuing him and his uniform was the same as that of Grew's, but they were still uncertain.

"Howdy, Lieutenant Grew," Pryor said, pushing the dun close to the white on which Grew sat, frowning at him.

They exchanged salutes. Grew, however, was wary. There were many spies and agents of the enemy roaming the country in uniform and late events had made Grew doubly cautious. Besides, it was fairly easy to steal an Army uniform, as Quantrell's men had proved.

"Say, George — look at this!" exclaimed the cowboy who had brought in the bay. "He's ours!"

A man with a healing scar on his cheek and a spot in his graying, sun-faded hair, turned clear blue eyes quickly on the bay. He was a heavy-bodied man, and his determined mouth showed that he had the qualities of leadership.

"You're right, Jake!" he growled. "I savvy that bay. I bought him from an Arikara in Oklahoma Territory! He's one of the hosses that Quantrell run off!"

The Rio Kid was now the object of all eyes, after the men had observed the recovered bay, but Pryor's attention was on Martin Grew. He liked the lean, efficient aspect of the young officer, in spite of his rather sad face. Many men in that time looked that way, however. Tragedy was common in the land.

Grew was a soldierly figure, clean, trim. Since the Rio Kid knew who Grew was, he was sure of himself. But neither Grew nor the cowmen with him as yet knew who the officer on the dun was.

"I'm Captain Bob Pryor, Lieutenant," the Rio Kid said, "and I'd thank yuh for a word in confidence."

Grew rode off a short distance with him, and the Rio Kid soon quieted Grew's natural suspicions of a stranger.

"Yore report reached General Grant hisself, Lieutenant," Pryor informed. "GHQ is interested in seein' Quantrell exterminated. I've come out to try to help do it."

Grew's eyes lighted. He shook hands heartily with Captain Pryor.

"I'm mighty glad you're here, Captain. These folks need help, and Quantrell has devastated the country. His guerrillas show no mercy and steal everything they can lay their hands on. I've been traveling through the section, buying horses, and just got back here yesterday. George Haven — he's the heavy-set man with the scar on his cheek — and his friends lost a bunch of mustangs to Quantrell. That bay is one of them!"

46

"And a Quantrell raider rode him," said Pryor. "I reckon the guerrillas wanted the mounts for this big attack. Lawrence is afire and they've shot down hundreds of citizens there."

Grew swore under his breath, frowning.

"These men would be glad of a chance to even the score with Quantrell. Suppose we head for the town? We were on our way there when we ran into you just now. These ranchers with me must have supplies in order to skin through, and retain their homes. The animals stolen by Quantrell meant everything to them."

The Rio Kid nodded. He understood how difficult the position of such people had become through the war.

"We'll keep it under our hats, just who I am, Grew, and why I'm here. You introduce me as Captain Pryor — that's plenty."

"Right."

Rejoining Haven and the other ranchers, the Rio Kid nodded to the Kansans. He liked their sturdy, honest appearance.

"Quantrell's in Lawrence in full force," Pryor told them. "There ain't enough of us to beat the guerrillas off, but we could help."

"Let's go, then," Haven growled.

They set their mounts toward the great smoke pall rising from the smitten, burning city, and rode along, following the Rio Kid and Grew toward Lawrence. The sun was high, and beating down fiercely upon them, the dust billowing from the beating hoofs, but any such discomfort went unnoticed.

At last, reaching the outskirts of the settlement, they found that Quantrell's men were retreating south, out of Lawrence, for at last resistance was mounting. The raiders had ravaged the city, however, setting swathes of fires that had gutted the lines of tinder-dry homes and stores.

The dead bodies of men, citizens and soldiers alike, lay in the gutters and on the wooden sidewalks. Frantic women and children ran about, seeking their loved ones.

Quantrell had brought in around four hundred tough, murderous guerrillas and they had done a thorough job. Now they were several miles south of Lawrence, harried by pursuing troops, but getting further and further away.

Skirting the hot flames in the center of the city, the Rio Kid and Lieutenant Grew, trailed by Haven's group, sought to overtake the van and get into the scrap before Quantrell and his men should get away entirely. The dun was swift and carried Pryor out ahead of the rest.

Along the dirt road out of Lawrence lay

the bodies of horses and more Kansans, with only here and there a dead guerrilla. The victims attested to the snarling fury and accuracy of Quantrell's guns, for every man who rode with Quantrell was a genius with a Colt, and trained in point-blank shooting from a running horse.

Now the fleeing guerrillas were well-mounted, thanks to the raid they had made on Haven's ranch, and they were able to keep out ahead of the poorly organized pursuit. The few pursuers who dared ride on their heels too closely were attacked and shot down by ravening, dead-shot guerrillas.

The Rio Kid, flashing along on Saber, noted the terrible sign posts — corpses of those who had pressed Quantrell and had received guerrilla lead for their pains. He came to a small rise, where a skirmish had evidently taken place between the running raiders and a company of raw, half-trained troopers from the Army camp. Thirty soldiers lay in a ragged line on the plain, with several horses about them. Quantrell's men had turned and charged here — and had won.

The sun was reddening to Pryor's right as he pressed on. Reaching the van of the Army forces chasing the guerrillas, Pryor found a major in charge.

He reported, offering his help.

"They're splitting up," the officer growled. "The country's broken up and wooded ahead. Cap'n, Quantrell's as clever as a fox."

These men, brave fighters as they were, felt awe for the terrific striking power of the guerrillas, for their ruthlessness. Pushed too hard now, however, Quantrell had given the order to his men to break into a hundred or more small bands. Those bands diverged with as many trails into the woods and chaparral of rising hills. They were swinging southeast, back into Missouri from whence they had come for the horrible attack.

Night overtook the Rio Kid and the Union forces in the van. Quantrell had escaped.

CHAPTER V
PURSUIT

Ruin and death in Lawrence had been frightful. Hundreds had died and over a million dollars worth of damage had been done by the fires set by Quantrell. Wanton destruction, it might be called, with revenge as a motive. For Quantrell hated Lawrence above other places, since it was there he had been first outlawed, and there where he had been accused of some of his uncounted crimes.

The whole state lay under a pall of horror because of this latest raid by the guerrillas. It was unbelievable, yet Quantrell had brought it off, and had escaped with all of his men who had not been killed — and his dead were comparatively few.

The day following the pillaging of Lawrence, the Rio Kid rode to George Haven's ranch. He had picked up Grew and his friends on the back trail.

Arrived there, the debonair Pryor, who

had an eye for feminine beauty, did not miss the lovely girl standing at the side of the house. It had been quickly repaired after the burning the night Quantrell had run off the horses. Sod bricks were to be had for the cutting, and Martin Grew had helped out, as had Haven's neighbors.

A huge man in Union blue, with a major's insignia on his tunic saluted the two youthful officers as Grew and Pryor dismounted. Haven and his rancher friends were pulling into the yard, and there were women about, too — wives and daughters of the settlers who had collected at the H Bar.

The Rio Kid noted the way the girl's violet eyes lighted when she saw Martin Grew, and the sudden smile which touched Grew's sad features as he greeted her.

"I'll eat my hat if they ain't sweet on each other," he decided. "Grew has mighty good taste. She's shore a beauty."

"This is Miss Edith Haven, Cap'n," Grew was saying then. "And Major Thompson, may I present Cap'n Robert Pryor?"

"Howdedo, Captain," Thompson cried in his bull voice.

Pryor took in the major. He was breathtakingly large, and had thick lips, Burnside whiskers which were the latest rage, and a massive head with curly, iron-gray hair.

Myriad wrinkles around his deep-set blue eyes were set into play as he smiled and nearly broke Pryor's hand with his grip.

The Rio Kid learned that the women and children had been brought to the H Bar for safety's sake, when so many of their men had set off for Lawrence. Half a score of older settlers were on guard over them. Bob Pryor met the wives and daughters of the settlers, especially the wife and two younger children of Milt Young of the Star 2. He also met Jake Phillips and the injured Ben, his brother, whom he knew at once as transplanted Texans, from their raw-boned look and their red skins. Bewhiskered Pop Schultz was in charge of the home guard. He was ancient, stocky and wide, and his beard was white. His near-sighted eyes blinked merrily, however.

"Hey, boys — what luck?" was the first thing Schultz had sung out to the weary men when they rode in.

George Haven muttered a curse as he dismounted from his dusty horse, a spavined animal which was the best left on his ranch by Quantrell.

"Any chance we had of gettin' a loan from the bank," Haven reported, "was finished by Quantrell. He raided Lawrence yestidday, folks, and looted and burnt the town.

Killed around a thousand people, they reckon. I talked with Herb Ince, of the bank. He says that even if Quantrell hadn't took all the cash they had that they weren't puttin' out no more loans this year. Things are too uncertain."

"Huh!" Pop remarked with a shrug of his hunched, wide shoulders. "Well, we'll have to eat grass then, till next season."

Major Thompson pulled at one of his sideburns, a look of concern wiping the smile from his face.

"I wish I could help you folks," he said earnestly. "Haven — Pop — I think I could sell some land for yuh, if yuh need cash. Land ain't much account right now but I'd like to give yuh a boost."

Haven blinked. "I dunno, Major. Mebbe I'll take yuh up, if yuh can get any sort of price. Things are mighty bad. I could head west and stake out another claim, I reckon."

"I hate to quit," muttered Pop.

These men were all desperate. Their reserves were all gone, and they had little food left. Most of their animals before had been run off by other raiders, and when the horses on which they had staked their fortunes had been stolen by Quantrell their last chance was gone.

"Quantrell's got to be set by his heels,

sooner or later," Lieutenant Grew growled. "He's done more damage and caused more misery than any man ever known in these parts."

"You're right, Lieutenant." Major Thompson nodded. "I'd give my right arm to lay hands on that scoundrelly guerrilla. In fact, I've been huntin' him for a year, but he's as slippery as an eel. Once I did come up with him, at the head of three hundred troopers — but do yuh think we took him? Nope. He got plumb away, durin' the darkness, after we'd fought all day.

"He was holed up in a farmhouse and I lost half my men in the fight. Then Quantrell and Todd and his cronies made a run for it at night. I was nearly broke for that, but got let off with a right hand dressin'-down. A good many others have run into the same kind of trouble when they've tried to arrest Quantrell."

The major's voice was rueful as he confessed his defeat.

"I'll never forgive Quantrell," he said grimly. "I'll run him to earth if it's the last thing I do."

The Rio Kid listened. He was sorry for the settlers, but his first duty was to go after the guerrillas.

"Where yuh reckon he's headed to this

time, Major?" he asked.

"Who — Quantrell?" said Thompson. "Why, the Missouri thickets, of course. He always does."

The Rio Kid spent the rest of the afternoon and the night at the H Bar. Saber needed attention and rest as much as Pryor did himself, and in the ranch corral the dun grazed and recovered his power, after the long run on Quantrell's trail.

Pryor learned as much as the settlers could tell him of the guerrillas' habits, and at the same time grew acquainted with the Kansans and their pressing problems of life. He wished he could give them a hand in their trouble.

Early next day, with Grew at his side, he rode to Lawrence, arriving about noon.

Captain Edward Terrell had reached the town that morning, with a force of crack cavalry, and the Rio Kid located him, reporting what he had learned.

"We got here too late," Terrell said ruefully. "This is by far the biggest and worst of Quantrell's raids, Pryor."

Grew was introduced to Terrell. Then the three officers discussed their next move, on Quantrell's trail.

"It's up to me," said the Rio Kid. "I'll head on Quantrell's trail, Cap'n, and try to locate his hideout. In the meantime operate as yuh see fit but leave me word here and at Baxter Springs, in the south near the Missouri line, where to find yuh. I'll send word back soon as possible. I reckon the guerrillas'll meet at some regular place in Missouri, not too far from the Border. If I circulate around in disguise mebbe I'll find where."

"That's all right," agreed Terrell. "Except I don't think Quantrell'll go to Missouri this time. He might after an ordinary raid, but I have a hunch it'll be different this time."

"Why?"

"Well, it's not so easy now. The Confederates are in a shaky position in the West, and then this attack on Lawrence has stirred up the whole nation. Thousands of fightin' men are coming to this point, thirstin' for Quantrell's blood."

"Where will he go then, yuh reckon?" asked the Rio Kid.

Terrell shrugged. "I can't say. He may turn east into Kentucky or then he might cross the Territory into Texas."

"I'll check up when I reach the Line," said the Rio Kid.

He took leave of Terrell and Grew and, ready for a long run, mounted the dun and headed southeast for Missouri, the direction in which the guerrillas had started their retreat. Quantrell was a fox, so far as hiding his whereabouts went, and the Rio Kid took to heart Captain Terrell's warning.

He was riding on the trail of the worst killer the country had ever known, a man who would cut his heart out without the slightest compunction, for a jest. . . .

It was hot as the days passed, a dry heat that drew all the moisture from man and beast. And as the Rio Kid rode the winding red clay trail through the woods, his dun was plastered with the sticky earth.

The scout was alert, his eyes always flicking from point to point, for he was in the wilderness. Not only were there likely to be stray enemy soldiers and outlaws in these parts, but there were roving bands of Indians, made bold by the war the white men were fighting. The redmen were ever ready to pounce upon a lone traveler.

The usually debonair Rio Kid, the spruce Army officer, was completely obliterated now by the disguise he had assumed in his pursuit of William Clarke Quantrell, the guerrilla chieftain, and by layers of varicolored dusts which he had picked up in the regions through which he had passed. He had not shaved for a week, and the stubble stuck out like wire, while his red-rimmed eyes, irritated by the brilliant sunlight of the South and by grit, gleamed from narrowed pits.

All in all, with nondescript clothing, old leather chaps, a battered "Nebraska" flat-topped Stetson, and a torn, butternut shirt, with a tobacco tag dangling from the open pocket, the Rio Kid looked like a real desperado. But his Colts were ready in the cartridge belts that circled his lean waist. And under his shirt he carried two more revolvers in shoulder holsters.

With this small arsenal, in a scrap he could deliver twenty shots without having to stop and reload. In addition, a carbine rode in its sling under one cocked leg, while his saddlebags bulged with provisions.

The Rio Kid had arrested many looters and deserters from both armies during the Civil War and he had had no trouble in disguising himself to look like one.

So far, the trail had proved long and disappointing. Quantrell and his men had split up, and nothing had been seen of them in their usual haunts in Missouri. Still, by spending plenty of money on whiskey, filling up natives to loosen tongues, Pryor had finally come upon a slight clue. A Missourian had remarked that he had seen a couple of Quantrell's followers riding toward the Territory — Indian Territory — and because of this the Rio Kid had swung southwest.

The narrow road he now was traveling dipped down into a wooded valley, through which a creek flowed. As the trail widened and turned, the Rio Kid saw a small settlement ahead — a few rough log cabins on the east bank of the stream and a large place which probably was a saloon and inn. The Rio Kid rode on toward the place.

Weary, and discouraged by the almost impossible task he had set himself, he slowed Saber and swung toward the saloon. It was a rambling, one-story affair, with a stable at the rear. It had narrow loophole windows, but the door stood open because of the heat. He heard the sound of men's voices from inside and smelled raw liquor and frying food.

There was a pump in the side yard and he led the dun around, washed him down with buckets of water, and gave him a light drink.

"Oh, yuh still got fight in yuh, have yuh?" he murmured, as Saber snorted and rolled his mirled eye toward some tethered horses. "Well, yuh can't tear into them mustangs. Yuh got to behave."

There were half a dozen other horses in

the shade at the rail along the log wall of the saloon, saddled horses. The Rio Kid had started to lead the dun on past, so that Saber would not be able to reach any of them and start a fuss, when his alert eye suddenly took in the brand on a buckskin gelding's flank.

"H Bar!" he muttered, and it hit him hard.

He kept on going, after a swift glance at the other horse. It was a powerful, handsome beast, the mustang strain mixed with Arab blood giving it size. The tail was lighter than the animal's hide and it bared its teeth and lashed out at Saber as the dun snorted in passing. The saddle on the buckskin was sweated.

"H Bar!"

The brand on a horse was not usually run over or switched, as was that on a cow. Bills-of-sale established ownership and the original brand remained on the animal. If Haven had lost this buckskin to Quantrell, then —

The implication seemed plain.

CHAPTER VI
A BRAND POINTS THE WAY

Leaving the dun in the shade, away from the other horses, the Rio Kid strode around to the door of the saloon. As he entered, he was blinded by the sudden transition into the gloom of the interior after the sunlight, but only for the first few moments.

Silence fell while the drinkers eyed the stranger. There was a crude bar to the right, Pryor saw as his eyes grew accustomed to the dimness, one made of a plank resting on upended logs. Another plank served as a counter on which bottles of whiskey and glasses stood.

The floor was the stamped dirt. There were three home-made tables on which lay decks of greasy cards. Two men at one table were silently playing, while several others lined the bar, drinking whiskey.

"Native pizen," ordered the Rio Kid breezily.

He meant to act the desperado, brash and

ready for trouble, but first he must get acclimated.

Nobody said anything for a time. Then a brawny, wide-bodied fellow who sported a black fan beard and who had rather small, shiny black eyes peering over his whiskers asked the barman:

"How far is it to Sulphur Spring, hombre?"

"Yuh mean in Texas?"

"Yeah, Texas. Sulphur Spring. How far?"

"Yuh foller this road after it crosses the crik," the bartender told him judicially, "and then yuh'll hit a bigger trail that swings south, mebbe ten mile on. Stay on her till yuh come to Sulphur Spring but don't ride too fast. Yuh might go right through without savvyin' yuh're there. It's a full day's ridin' — fifty, sixty mile."

The man with the black fan beard nodded and, picking up his glass, drained it off.

"Gimme one of them Cuba ropes," he ordered briskly, pointing to the box of cigars.

"I got a hoss," remarked the Rio Kid loudly, "that can out-run any animile south of the Mason-Dixon Line, and that's the best in the world, gents."

Every man pricked up his ears. Horse races were the commonest forms of diversions, and each man possessed a mustang he would take an oath could beat any other.

"There's a buckskin out there and my horse can run him ragged," Pryor boasted. "He's the best on the line."

"How much money could yuh put on that?" the man with the black fan whiskers asked quietly.

"So he's yores," thought the Rio Kid, without a flicker. He drew a bag of silver from his pocket and clinked it on the bar.

"Barkeep can hold the stakes," he announced.

Everybody, including the bartender, went outside to watch the race. The little black eyes quickly sized up the bony dun. A look of calculating joy came into the brawny fellow's face. The dun was none too prepossessing in appearance and the buckskin seemed a much better horse. Both animals were dusty and had been ridden hard, so it was even. Besides, this was to be a dash.

"Around that big gray rock and back to the door," said Blackbeard.

A revolver fired in the air started them off. It was from a stop, and the buckskin spurted away. The black-whiskered man was a fine rider. Saber instantly realized it was a race, though, and his long legs flashed into action as he was urged on by the soft voice of his rider, low over his neck.

The buckskin made the turn on a dead heat but had the inner track, and Saber skidded around. He heard the Rio Kid's voice begging him to run, and put all he had into the return to the saloon door. He came in half a length ahead of the swift buckskin, and a cheer rose.

"Yore money, hombre," the barkeeper said, handing the stakes to Pryor.

The loser looked chagrined. He cast a glance on the deceptive dun that could run with the speed of the wind.

"That's the first time Buck was ever beat," he growled.

"Well, drinks are on me," Pryor said cheerfully. "Better luck next time."

Having identified the man who was riding the buckskin, the Rio Kid was pleased that he had no trouble at all in coaxing the man to the bar. In fact, the brawny fellow was disposed to linger and trade drink for drink. He had plenty of money on him, even though he had lost in the horse race. He was pleasant and smiling, and told a couple of coarse jokes that brought guffaws from the house.

"Yuh're a man after my own heart, hombre," he cried, slapping Pryor on the back after the third round of whiskies. "Call me

Blackie. What'll I call you?"

"Bob — Kentucky Bob," answered Pryor.

"Right, Bob. Yore hoss is all right and so're you. Set 'em up again, bartender."

"He's shore lovin'," thought the Rio Kid. "Now why —"

It came out after a time. Mellowed by whiskey, Blackie said:

"Well, I must be gettin' on. Bob, why not ride a ways with me?"

"Which way yuh goin'? I'm headin' for the Pecos sooner or later, Blackie."

"Then we can keep each other company," Blackie said. "One more and we'll start."

The Rio Kid feigned to be somewhat befuddled by the whiskey. He had a hunch, now, what Blackie's game might be. If the man was a horse-thief, then Saber would attract him with a tremendous lure. Such speed of hoof would spell life or death for a man in the trade he was certain was Blackie's.

"A hundred to one he's after Saber," he decided.

But he wished to stay with Blackie, the best clue he had yet come upon in his search for Quantrell.

Paying up, and smoking Cuban stogies, they went out and mounted, the Rio Kid purposely staggering a bit and fumbling

66

with his reins. He wanted Blackie to think the drinks had him.

Splashing across the rocky, shallow ford of the red-watered creek, they climbed the west bank and found the road, a two-wheel track that wound through the brush, with sandy, pinkish soil under the horses' hoofs.

They kept on for three miles after the little saloon was out of sight and earshot behind them. They were not far from the Texas line now, and the country was utterly deserted, wild with chaparral and broken, rocky hills.

"Dog it!" exclaimed Blackie, slowing his buckskin. "There goes that cussed cinch buckle again!"

"He ain't losin' any time," thought the Rio Kid.

He kept on a few paces, as from the corner of one eye he saw Blackie dismounting on the far side of the buckskin. That, of course, was to hide his hand when he drew his Colt. The first shot, the Rio Kid knew, would be aimed for his head or upper body, as Blackie was after the dun and would not wish to injure the swift, valuable beast.

His keen ear caught the slight click as Blackie, squatted by his horse, pulled his Colt and cocked it to fire under the buckskin.

Instantly he threw himself off Saber.

Blackie's shot whirled a foot over his head. As he hit the sand, the Rio Kid had his pistol in hand, the hammer spur back under his thumb. He had to shoot to kill, for Blackie was dangerous. He had no doubt now that he had run into one of Quantrell's guerrillas.

As an echo, the Rio Kid's Colt exploded. He fired under Buck's long belly at the crouched Blackie who, seeing he had somehow missed his first, was swinging swiftly to pin him. The Rio Kid's slug whipped into the bunched-up body striking the vitals, and Blackie rolled over on his side, his revolver exploding as he went.

The gunny's second bullet bit a chunk of hide from the buckskin's belly, stinging him frightfully. The big horse screeched, reared high and came down running at full-tilt. He flashed away from there and galloped wildly on the back-trail. Blackie lay where he had fallen, doubled up in a ball like a curled porcupine, but he had no stings left. His dark eyes were glazing and his mouth wide, gasping.

The Rio Kid carefully checked him, removing his fangs, and confiscated Blackie's Colts. He went through the burly man's pockets hunting clues but found only money, Union cash, no doubt stolen in the

Lawrence raid.

"Yuh on yore way to meet Quantrell, Blackie?" he growled, shaking the shuddering desperado.

Only by the quickening in the small black eyes did Pryor believe that he might have guessed right. He would have preferred to have accompanied Blackie on the trail and reach the rendezvous, which he figured might be at Sulphur Spring, Texas. It was to that spot that Blackie had been headed, anyway, judging by his inquiry of the bartender back at the saloon. But Blackie had made this impossible by coveting Saber.

Blackie was trying to say something. Pryor put his ears to the whispering lips.

"Pull — pull my boots off," he heard.

The Rio Kid obliged. Lots of tough fellows hated to die with their boots on.

"How 'bout Quantrell, Blackie? Is he at Sulphur Spring?"

Again he caught the flicker, knew he had made a hit. Blackie was again trying to speak, but when the Rio Kid bent and listened, he heard: "Cuss yuh! He'll carve yore heart out!"

Blackie shuddered, and flexed back. When he relaxed he was dead. The Rio Kid shrugged, seized the man's ankles and pulled him into the bush, leaving the body to the buzzards. Mounting, he rode on.

He slept a few hours in the chaparral after dark fell, but was up in the gray of the dawn. He ate cold beef and biscuit, watered the dun sparingly, and, washing up himself, pushed on through rolling, wild country.

He was in vast Texas, his home state, as big as many empires. Nostalgia seized him. He remembered his parents, his rancher father on the Rio Grande, his mother, whom he had not seen since leaving three years before to fight the War on the side of the North.

It had been a hard choice to make, for most of his boyhood friends and even his family were Confederate sympathizers. But Sam Houston, at the beginning of the fratricidal conflict, had spoken for the Union, and his voice had decided Pryor, torn between two devotions. Now Houston was dead, had laid down his saber the previous year, a tired old man. . . .

It was late the afternoon of the day following his brush with Blackie that the Rio Kid reached Sulphur Spring.

It was in the hills, a roost set near some big yellow-watered pools that bubbled from the raw red hills. Pines and spruce showed dark on the slopes, while chaparral covered the lower draws and ravines. It was wild, primitive land, filled with deer trails and Indian runs.

The building he saw as he rode up was surprisingly large, the only one in Sulphur Spring save for the surrounding sheds and the barn servicing it. It was made of native timber — pine logs morticed at the corners — and was rambling, set low, covering a good deal of ground with its side wings and lean-tos.

There were windows, although none had any glass in them. The northern ones were covered with greased paper, while shutters could be closed against the wintry blasts. However, it was hot now, and they were not needed.

The crude sign over the bar entrance spelled out:

JAKE'S ONLY CHANCE

There were some unsaddled horses in a big woods corral to the rear. A spring wagon stood in the open-front shed, while the various accoutrements for riding and driving horses — saddles, leather harness, and so on — hung under the roof. Piles of tin cans, covered by swarms of black flies, were close to the kitchen door.

After tending the dun, the Rio Kid strode

through the open entry into the bar.

The place was crowded. The floor of stamped dirt was sprinkled with damp sawdust, from the woodpile in the rear. A bar with a small mirror over it was to the left, and tables and rude chairs were scattered about.

Two men were serving drinks, one in a dirty apron, the other in his shirt sleeves. The latter was a stout, bland-faced fellow who evidently was the proprietor. He wore a cartridge belt with a reversed Colt in it.

Perhaps thirty armed fellows were in the big room. They were lounging about, playing cards or drinking. A few were just sitting or standing with their glasses in hand.

Every man was armed to the teeth with pistols, knives, and crossed cartridge belts, while many had carbines or double-barreled shotguns leaning close at hand. Some were clean, others dirty and unshaven, according to each one's desire.

All eyes turned on the stranger, the Rio Kid. In his get-up as a Texas desperado, he hoped nothing was amiss.

Blinking from the strong light, the Rio Kid stepped to the bar.

"Mighty dry ridin'," he remarked. "Let's have it."

The stout, bland-looking innkeeper served

him, accepting the silver dollar he rang on the bar.

"Come far?" he asked pleasantly.

"Huh? Oh, yeah. I did."

The Rio Kid deliberately eyed him as he drank. Such curiosity was not welcome in Texas.

"No offense, no offense. Stayin' long?"

Pryor frowned. "As long as I do," he growled.

Somebody snickered and the bartender turned a shade redder. He cleared his throat, but then, seizing a dirty cloth, began wiping the top of the plank.

A man came through a rear doorway into the main saloon.

"Jesse," the man called, "was that Blackie who came in?"

The Rio Kid's eyes swung to him.

The fellow stood about six feet, and his figure was sinewy and well-formed. He had a pleasant face, with a big hooked nose, and his crisp hair grew luxuriant about his well-shaped head. His blue eyes were sharp and penetrating. The eyebrows were thick, while a carefully tended mustache curled over his firm, wide mouth. About him was the vigorous air of a leader.

"No, Chief," a youth replied. " 'Twasn't Blackie."

The Rio Kid did not dare to stare too long at the big man in the rear of the saloon. He knew now that he had come up with Quantrell, the murderous guerrilla, and a band of his close associates, and he had to move warily.

CHAPTER VII
ROBBERS' ROOST

Heatedly and fluently, Quantrell cursed.

"How long does that fool Blackie think I'll wait?" Pryor heard him exclaim.

The guerrilla chieftain was plainly impatient. Blackie, the Rio Kid deduced, must have been carrying some sort of information, perhaps about the situation back in Missouri, to Quantrell.

"So this is where he holed up!" mused the Rio Kid, careful not to show any curiosity or interest in Quantrell or in the surrounding guerrillas.

There was a brooding, but tense atmosphere in the saloon. They were watching the stranger in their midst and if they had the slightest suspicion of him they would kill him. In fact, at a whim they would riddle him with lead, just for sport, if they felt that way.

He was near the open door but such men were the most expert shots in the country, with pistol. If they attacked him he might kill two or three, but with so many determined opponents he would die before he made the exit. It took the steeliest nerve to show not the faintest sign of excitement but to keep on with his drink.

Quantrell, who was in his bare feet — he had left his spurred boots in the back where he had been resting — came over to the bar and had a quick drink. The stout proprietor slid down the bar and spoke to him in an undertone, and Quantrell looked up toward the Rio Kid.

Presently the guerrilla chief walked over and stood beside Bob Pryor.

"Good afternoon," said Quantrell in a quiet, pleasing voice. "Rather warm, ain't it?"

"Reckon it is."

"Yuh come in from the east, I hear," said Quantrell. "Did yuh happen to pass a rider with a black beard, prob'ly on a buckskin hoss? A friend of mine."

The Rio Kid understood that he could not answer Quantrell as he had squelched the bartender.

"No, I didn't," he answered civilly. "Mebbe he was on the other trail. I come up from the south fork."

"I see. Thanks."

Quantrell sniffed. He hesitated a moment, looked sharply at the Rio Kid and his get-up, then shrugged, murmured a "So long," and went back through the door out of sight.

"It's yore play, Cole," said the fresh-faced youth whom Quantrell had addressed as "Jesse." "Come on. I'm goin' to scalp yuh on this one."

Pryor had taken care to memorize some of the more prominent names in Quantrell's main band.

"That must be Jesse James, that kid," he decided. "And that hombre he calls Cole must be one of the Younger boys."

Jesse James, still in his 'teens but a tried and trusted member of Quantrell's elite, had a smooth, youthful face. His sparkling blue eyes were merry. He was tall and well-built, and carried his guns with a careless nonchalance and dash. He wore buckskin pants and shirt, but the hat cocked on the side of his handsome head once had belonged to a Union officer, and no doubt had been taken from the murdered owner.

Cole Younger was also a fine-looking specimen of manhood. A tall, powerful youth, he had an intelligent face and a commanding appearance. His Missouri drawl as he jested with Jesse James was that of an educated man.

A slender but solid fellow, carrying a leather strap he had just been mending, came through the front door, and went to Jesse James. His narrow face was bearded, his blue eyes were somber, and his thin lips did not smile.

"Still foolin' with that strap, Frank?" asked Cole Younger. "Yuh'll turn into a leather mender soon."

"I can't fix the blame thing. Jesse, see can you do it."

Jesse James paused in his game to help his brother, Frank James. Frank was four years older, and he had lost any youthful joy he might ever have felt in living.

The Rio Kid was well aware of the dangerous characters of the men he was trailing. But peril was a tonic to him, and he knew that he must make a bold attempt to open some sort of connection with the Quantrell gang. He raised his whiskey glass and said, loudly and truculently:

"Here's to Jeff Davis, and blast the Yankees!"

The guerrillas were Southern sympathizers, according to their lights, even though the Confederacy had been appalled by their bloodthirsty exploits. Jeff Davis had refused Quantrell any official recognition such as a commission, horrified by the massacres the guerrilla chief had perpetrated.

Quantrell had used the Civil War as an excuse to satisfy his murderous, revengeful nature. The awful raid on Lawrence had been made because the law in Lawrence had sought to arrest Quantrell for thievery and murders committed before the outbreak of hostilities.

A sudden silence fell as the Rio Kid called the toast to the President of the C.S.A.

"S'pose," a voice said after a moment, "we don't feel like drinkin', hombre?"

It was Jesse James who had spoken. His sparkling blue eyes were fixed on the Rio Kid. Pryor's thoughts raced. He knew that these fellows approved the toast, and so he took a chance. Jesse James was smiling.

"I said, 'Here's to Jeff Davis!' " He scowled, glass up.

Jesse James broke into a shout of laughter, and drank with the rest.

"Yuh got yore nerve with yuh, rooster," James said. "Now it's my turn: May they all rot in perdition, and Kansas longest of all!"

The Rio Kid drank with the rest. Then the toasts flew thick and fast. Profane, violent, the guerrillas expressed their hate of their foes.

As dark fell, the gathering grew more mellow. The Rio Kid found little difficulty in exchanging drinks with Jesse James and Cole Younger. Sure of themselves, the two feared no man. And here they were surrounded by their trusted comrades and far from any possible Federal soldiers.

Feigning to be overcome somewhat by the strong drink, the Rio Kid, in his character as a Border desperado, let his tongue loosen. He boasted, guardedly, of Yankee soldiers he had killed, and of his supposed battles against the Federals. Topping him, Jesse James and Cole Younger, with whom he had taken a seat, described some of their own forays.

Hour after hour passed. The air of the saloon was thick with malodorous tobacco smoke which hung about the hot chimneys of the lighted oil lamps. A couple of men had rolled off their seats and lay, snoring on the sawdust.

Finally the Rio Kid leaned back against the wall, his head lolling on his chest. Apparently he was asleep.

Younger glanced at him and then at Jesse James. Both were heavy with liquor. Pryor caught Cole's whisper:

"What yuh think of him, Jesse?"

"He's all right," James replied. "The kind of hombre the chief can use."

"I think so, too. Wonder what the boss

expects to do next? That Lawrence affair ought to blowed over some by now."

"He's awful close-mouthed when he's plannin' somethin'," Jesse James said. "Wonder what happened to Blackie Frone? He was s'posed to fetch Quantrell a report."

"I dunno. But from the latest I heard, the Federals was after us as thick as hives of bees, Jesse. The war ain't goin' as well as it might, for us."

A heavy step sounded from the rear. Under one lash, the Rio Kid saw Quantrell, hurrying from the back of the building. He was wearing riding boots and spurs, and a Stetson was strapped to his thick-haired head. The insignia he sported was that of a Union major, and the jacket and rest of the uniform was a Federal officer's. No doubt it had been taken from some victim of Quantrell.

Frank James and three other guerrillas, in various Federal blue uniforms, followed Quantrell.

"Good-night, boys," Quantrell said to them. "I can't wait any longer for Blackie. Todd has the orders."

The guerrilla chieftain hurried outside, and in a few moments the Rio Kid caught the rapid retreating hoofs of horses. The riders were headed eastward, back toward Missouri and Kansas, as far as he could tell.

It was impossible for him to rush out, saddle up, and trail Quantrell in the darkness. This would rouse the guerrillas' suspicion instantly, even if he could stick on such men as Quantrell and Frank James at night, close enough to keep them in earshot.

Chagrined at seeing his prize leave the spot, after such trouble expended to track him there, the Rio Kid still had to pretend sleep. He decided that his remaining chance was in staying with Jesse James and Younger. Quantrell must be planning a campaign, and Todd, his lieutenant, would eventually, lead the bulk of the guerrillas to the rendezvous arranged.

Soon the lamps were blown out. Many of the guerrillas retired to the back of the inn to sleep. The Rio Kid quietly lay down near the bench, sleeping through the night in the sawdust.

Jesse James grinned at him in the morning. He was certain that Pryor had been in a stupor.

The smell of frying food was appetizing, and after breakfast, purchased from the hotel keeper and consumed in the company of Jesse and Cole Younger, the Rio Kid felt he must make a pretense of being on his way.

"I reckon I better be ridin', boys," he said, "but I shore enjoyed yore company. 'Tain't often a man runs into fellers with the same sort of ideas he has hisself."

He waited, hoping against hope, and caught the quick glance the two guerrillas exchanged. Then Jesse James said:

"Yore object in life is to kill as many Feds as possible, ain't it, Bob?"

The Rio Kid had told them to call him "Kentucky Bob," the same nickname he had made up for Blackie Frone.

"Yeah."

"Well, travel with us a while and yuh'll not be disappointed. Ain't I right, Cole?"

"Yes, suh," Younger declared.

The Rio Kid pretended to hesitate.

"I had an idee of doin' some business acrost the Pecos," he finally said. "It's gettin' hot in the States right now."

"Are yuh afraid?" James growled.

"Shore not. But yuh'll have to guarantee I'll see action, and pronto. I ain't the kind of man to loll around idle."

"Come outside a minute," ordered Cole Younger.

The tall guerrilla led the way into the sunshine. It was still cool from the night, but the sun was growing warmer in the blue sky of Texas.

"See that cottonwood sprig over there?" Younger said to the Rio Kid. "Watch it."

He drew his six-shooter and, without apparently aiming, fired the gun. The little sapling whipped violently, and showed the mark of the slug with a chunk of bark ripped off. In reply, Pryor drew a Colt and shot on the flash. The tip of the cottonwood flew off as his bullet hit.

Jesse James, watching the match, chuckled with delight.

"I knowed he could handle a Colt, Younger!" he exclaimed. "Yuh can tell it to look at his hands. The chief'll be plumb tickled."

Cole Younger slapped Pryor on the back.

"Yuh're hired, Bob, if yuh say so. Yuh'll have a bellyful of fightin' if yuh travel our trail."

"Yeah? What's the pay?"

"Hosses, ammunition, and all yuh can take. Look!" Younger drew a big money bag from inside his shirt and jingled it. "More'n any man can spend."

"I'm with yuh," Pryor said promptly.

"Good. Yuh won't regret it."

Having allowed the two desperadoes to talk him into what he had wished to do all along, and now was considered a recruit to Quantrell's band, the Rio Kid had only to continue playing his assumed role. It should be easier from now on for him, for the initial opening had been the most difficult.

Jesse James was good-humored and easy to get along with, while the others accepted the Rio Kid on James' and Younger's say-so. But for two days, with the Rio Kid inwardly chafing for action, desiring to be after Quantrell, the gang stuck at the tavern in the wilds of Texas.

Then, without warning, at dawn one morning Jesse James started the Rio Kid awake, bending over him.

"Rise and shine," Jesse ordered. "We're ridin', Kentucky."

After a hurried breakfast, forty guerrillas, including the new recruit, the Rio Kid, alias "Kentucky Bob," saddled up. With Quantrell's lieutenant, George Todd at their head, they rode off. Todd cold, deadly, a fury in a fight, led them eastward back toward the fields of action.

The burly, scowling Todd was a terrible killer, who would roar into battle with a ferocity equalled only by that of the quieter but no less deadly Quantrell. The Rio Kid knew that — but he held himself ready for grim action.

Chapter VIII
Discovery

Quantrell had more followers than the picked men who had gone with him to hide in the Texas hinterland. The Rio Kid was assured that other groups would come to the appointed rendezvous at the proper time when they were needed.

The road back was over about the same route the Rio Kid had followed on his way down. They paused for a drink at the little tavern where Pryor had had the horse-race with Blackie Frone, but the Rio Kid was able to stay out of sight of the proprietor. He feared the man might recognize him and mention the race and Blackie.

Headed for Missouri under George Todd, the guerrillas pulled in one dark evening to some woods outside a village which, Jesse James told Pryor, was near the Kansas line.

More guerrillas waited for them at the bivouac and among them was Frank James. Pryor did not see Quantrell.

The camp was hidden in the trees and brush by the side of a creek. A hot meal of coffee, beef, potatoes and bread was prepared. And here the guerrillas rested after the long run from Texas.

Gossip immediately began between the two bands, as they compared experiences since the mass raid on Lawrence. Tales of bloodshed and daring escapes from Federal patrols filled the air.

The Rio Kid listened closely. Quantrell was his chief quarry and he hoped to come up with the guerrilla chief again. Once he could pin Quantrell in a spot for a long enough time to bring up Captain Terrell, the Rio Kid would strike. But he could not afford to make any mistake. Quantrell's hair-breadth escapes on previous occasions when it had seemed he was trapped made Pryor determined to nail the chief for good this time.

"Yuh'll have to see Quantrell, in the mornin'," Jesse James told him when the talk had gone on for a time. "He questions every man who jines his band. But don't worry. I'll put in a word for yuh, Bob."

George Todd, dipping chunks of hard bread into steaming coffee, was conversing in undertones with Frank James. The presence of the older James boy made the Rio

Kid fairly certain that Quantrell was in the neighborhood, and now what Jesse James said seemed to confirm it.

After supper, the tired raiders lay down in their blankets, drawn off from the fire. Among them was Bob Pryor, well on his way to becoming a trusted recruit of Quantrell's, whom he meant to arrest when the auspicious moment arrived.

He started awake some time later. Judging by the fire, which had died down to a few red embers, he decided it must be around midnight. A rider had just come into the camp, and the Rio Kid, lying on one side, watched the dim figure moving in the faint light.

Then a second man rode up, dismounted, and followed the first. There were sentries on duty, but they only saluted. The first man paused by the fire, stooped and lit a pine splinter which he touched to a cigar he meant to smoke. As the flare came up, the Rio Kid recognized Quantrell.

Quantrell walked on past the fire. A few paces behind him came the dark form of the cape-clad second horseman.

The two went to the rocks lying about under a bluff, and sat down. The Rio Kid could see the ruby glow of Quantrell's cheroot as the guerrilla chief drew on it, sitting near the black shadows of the under-brush.

Not only did curiosity burn in the Rio Kid's brain but he thought that if he could once overhear some of Quantrell's future plans he might set a trap from which the guerrillas could not escape. Edging from his blanket, he inched into the timber. The trees were small pines, for the most part, and the needles afforded him a quiet path under his hands and knees as he crept toward the spot where Quantrell sat.

It took him some minutes to come to a spot near enough to make out the words spoken by the two hunched, dark figures. Quantrell's face was toward him — he could tell that by the burning cigar in the guerril-la's lips. He missed the opening of the talk, but it was in the nature of an argument, the other man trying to convince Quantrell of something. They spoke in low tones.

"— war's not going to last forever, Quan-trell! We must think of the future!"

"Yuh're right," the guerrilla growled. "Curse the Federals! They'll never let me rest."

"Yuh can rest if yuh have plenty of *dinero*. Go to Texas or Mexico or even South America if yuh want. Why not throw yore men into this, as quick as possible? There's only a dozen families, perhaps a hundred people, to think about. Get rid of 'em and we'll have thousands of acres of the best ranchin' land in Kansas. It could be done in a night — think of it! The company I form will be the front. You can hide out till we cash in. After this war, that land will be worth money. We can parcel it out and sell it or run it off in big lots. It's rich earth."

"It's too close to Lawrence. They'll be on the watch for me."

"Shucks! That'll make it easier! They'll never believe yuh'd dare come so near this quick, Quantrell."

There was something vaguely familiar in the low undertones of the man speaking to Quantrell. But the Rio Kid could not see his features, and was unable then to identify the voice.

"Well — all right," Quantrell said, after a period of deep thought. "Yuh reckon there's enough in it to pay us?"

"A million, I tell yuh!"

The other man drove home the argument as Quantrell let himself be convinced.

"I'll handle it all. Smash them fool ranchers and that's all you need do."

"Who are they, exactly? Name 'em so's we'll be shore to wipe them all out."

"First," the other man said eagerly,

"there's George Haven, the H Bar owner — that's where yuh took the hosses."

"Of course, I remember. That was a good job yuh put us on to."

"And this is a better one! Then there's Young's ranch, the Phillips place, Schultz' —"

With a start of horror, the Rio Kid realized that the ranchers Quantrell meant to exterminate were the very people he had met. They were Martin Grew's friends, and the Rio Kid had pitied them for their troubles and liked them for their virtues.

"I'll have to get warnin' through to Haven," he thought grimly.

"Better turn in," Quantrell was saying, with a yawn. "Spend the night, Jay?"

"I believe I better. My hoss picked up a stone when we was crossin' the creek."

They moved, and the Rio Kid began working back toward his blanket bed. Quantrell and his friend turned in on the other side of the big encampment. The piping of tree frogs and night insects, the low purl of the water on the stones of the streambed, the snores of sleeping men and the soft *thud-thud* of hoofs at the picket lines helped hide what faint sounds he made in returning to his place.

He fell asleep after a time. His last thought

was that his main duty was to his orders from U. S. Grant, to arrest Quantrell. But he knew he must get warning to Haven and his friends in time.

The dawn found the guerrilla camp stirring. Gray mists swirled from the creek, but it looked as though the day would be fair. Red sunrise showed through the tops of the trees.

The Rio Kid, with Jesse James and Cole Younger close to him, ate some breakfast. Then Jesse said:

"C'mon, we'll take yuh to the chief, Bob. Look sharp, now. He's a wise one."

They led him to the other side of the camp. Sentries were lounging on the rocks, and guns were stacked. The guerrillas kept their small-arms on them, however. Many wore nondescript uniforms, parts of Union or Confederate equipment taken on the battlefield.

Quantrell's steady, appraising eyes raised to fix the new recruit, Kentucky Bob. The guerrilla chief was sitting on a log with his back to a big spruce, a mug of coffee in one hand and a piece of hard bread in the other, as Jesse James ushered his candidate up.

"Chief, meet Kentucky Bob," James said. "He's all right. He'd like to jine this army of yores."

Quantrell's sharp blue eyes drilled into the Rio Kid.

"Where yuh from, my boy?" he asked in a paternal fashion.

"Kentucky, suh. I fit in the ranks for a time but it wasn't a fast enough killin' of Yankees to suit me."

"I hear yuh were on yore way to Texas when the boys met yuh."

"Yes, Chief. 'Peared to me I could do more damage down there."

Quantrell seemed to be seeking within himself the answer as to whether the new recruit should be inducted into the guerrilla band or shot for breakfast. He certainly would not permit a man who had grown so intimate with members of his army to ride away.

"Yuh're an ace shot, I understand. That's settled. Every man who rides with Quantrell must be. Yuh've got nerve — I can see that in yore gaze. Are yuh loyal?"

The terrible eyes bored to the depths of the Rio Kid's soul. He was playing a difficult role. The slightest false note might mean his doom, the end of the dangerous tether he was letting out in his attempt to ensnare Quantrell.

"Yes, suh. I will fight to tarnation and back
—"

Quantrell took his eyes off him and the spell broke. Somebody had come around the rock bluff from the picket line, leading a big black horse.

"Good mornin'," the man with the horse boomed. "I got that pebble out, Quantrell, and I must be ridin' at once. Hoofs —"

The Rio Kid, recognizing the voice as that of the man who had been speaking with Quantrell the previous night, turned to look.

The fellow was huge and he wore a blue uniform with a Federal major's insignia. Horrified, the Rio Kid stared straight into the deep-set, dark-blue eyes of Major Jarvis Thompson, the supposed Union officer he had met at Haven's ranch in Kansas.

An instant later he knew by the flash of Thompson's eyes that the spy had recognized him!

The huge Thompson was quick but the Rio Kid shaded him. For Bob Pryor's reactions were as swift as lightning flashes.

As Thompson's heavy jaw dropped, the Rio Kid acted. He had a few breaths of time, little fractions that meant the difference between life and death, and he seized upon them avidly.

All about him were the guerrillas, deadly

94

killers and ace shots, every one. Quantrell lounged within a few feet of him and Thompson stood there with the reins of his big black horse in hand, about to expose the Rio Kid. Death was certain. Quantrell would shoot him or string him up within minutes.

"You cussed Federal!" shouted the Rio Kid, and went streaking at Thompson.

The big man dropped the black's reins, falling back as his first words were drowned by the maddened shriek of the Rio Kid. His huge paw dropped to the Colt in its holster at his burly hip. He snatched the gun out, the hammer spur rising, back under his thumb.

The Rio Kid drew as he leaped at Thompson. His weapon flared and Thompson whipped around with a gasping curse, staggering, falling hard in the rocks. His gun flipped from his grip into the air, the ringing, sudden sound telling that the slug had struck the heavy weapon and knocked it from his hand.

That had saved him. The Rio Kid could not afford to turn and go after Thompson, and already the big fellow was rolling over behind a boulder.

Quantrell, Jesse James, and the other guerrillas, staring in amazement at this astounding, unexpected duel between two they thought friends, misinterpreted the set-to. That was what the Rio Kid had hoped they would when he had accused Thompson of being a Federal.

"Hey — stop — wait!" roared Quantrell, scrambling to his booted feet and holding up a hand. "Kentucky Bob — Thompson — quit it! He's no Fed, yuh fool! Put them guns down!"

With their jaws dropped, tricked by the Rio Kid's stratagem of pretending he thought Thompson a Union officer and foe, the guerrillas missed their best chance of killing the clever agent.

As for the Rio Kid, he was whistling shrilly, bars of an Army song:

Said the Big Black Charger to the Little White Mare

That was a call to Saber to come to him. Wherever the dun might be, in corral or barn, or on the loose, if he heard that song he would come when he could get free. Pryor had left him in a nearby corral, and Saber would jump the fence —

But he hadn't time to wait for his mount. Within seconds the true nature of the fight would become plain to Quantrell and his men.

Thompson was catching his breath that had been knocked from his lungs by the shock of the bullet which had stung his fingers. Bits of lead had spattered his cheeks and eyes, and he had been jolted by his fall and the necessity of protecting his hide from the Rio Kid. But he was howling the truth:

"Kill him, Quantrell! Shoot the dog! He's a spy — spy — spy!"

CHAPTER IX
CHECKED

Pryor's bullet whacked a chunk from the flinty rock behind which Thompson cowered. Thompson's shrieks filled the clearing where confusion ran riot.

The Rio Kid, Colt in hand, jaw set, had reached the big black which Thompson had led up. He seized the reins as the horse, startled by the yelling and gunfires, reared up.

An instant later, the Rio Kid had hit leather, clinching his powerful legs about the great charger. He jerked the black's head around and, low over the horse, sped away from the camp.

Turning in the saddle and raising his Colt, the Rio Kid tried for Quantrell, but the guerrilla chief's luck held. Between him and the Rio Kid now several of his men had jumped, and at last they were drawing their weapons. Pryor's whizzing bullets ripped into their flesh, but they protected Quantrell.

And then, when Quantrell at last understood Thompson's warning cries and comprehended the actual facts, he fell back behind a tree. Yanking his pistol, he shot after the retreating Rio Kid.

The black was in full motion, leaping forward out of Quantrell's bivouac with powerful, long strides. He had tremendous life quivering in him, and was a splendid runner. The Rio Kid lay along his back and neck, close to him, holding with his legs, one hand free to shoot as he gripped the beast's silky mane with his other.

"Fire!" roared Quantrell, his face scarlet with his fury as he realized how close he had come to being tricked, perhaps arrested by a Federal spy. "Kill him!"

Guerrillas were running from every corner of the camp, seizing shotguns, carbines, drawing their revolvers. As they aimed at him, the Rio Kid jerked the black's reins, swerving to the right as he made for the protection of a bluff. A sentry leaped up just ahead of him, gun pointed up. Pryor fired into him and he folded up. The black's shoulder knocked him violently back into the brush.

The volley had come as the Rio Kid

turned the black. The heavy *whoosh* of rifle and .45 slugs passed within a foot of his head, but others, stray ones, did not miss altogether. The mighty black gave a leap, shrieked, and fell dead in the trail.

Close to the turn, the Rio Kid landed on his hunched shoulders, rolling over and over, scrabbling for temporary safety. A howl of triumph rose in guerrilla throats as they saw him fall. The black lay stretched in the path, quivering his last.

Bullets cut the rocks and brush, the earth, as the zigzagging Rio Kid leaped around the rock bluff, his breath rasping in and out of his strained lungs. He was shaken from the fall, and two slugs had dealt him flesh wounds. There was blood on his left hand, and on his cheek.

"Take him — go after him, boys!" bellowed Quantrell.

Thompson, who had called himself a major in the Union Army was yelling for the Rio Kid's blood. Jesse James, the pleasant smile gone from his boyish, pink-cheeked face, had a revolver out and was headed for the man who had fooled him, tricked him into bringing him to Quantrell.

The Rio Kid gave a desperate whistle blast, one that penetrated over the smashing of the guns and the cursing shouts of the enemy. A shrill answering whinny gave him fresh hope, as the guerrillas started running after him on foot, believing him finished.

Saber came streaking across the other edge of the clearing, plunged into the brush and trees, and emerged close to his rider.

Protected from the ferocious and deadly guerrilla guns for a few moments by the protruding rocky bluff, Pryor ran out and leaped to the bare back of the dun. Holding Saber's mane with one hand and with his Colt snarling back at the running killers, he hit the trail away from there.

Quantrell saw at once that the tide had swung in his quarry's favor.

"Horses — pronto, mount!" shouted the chief. "After him!"

Some of the guerrillas kept coming, while others turned and ran back to the corral and picket lines, to fetch their mounts. But now there were many trees between the flying Rio Kid and his swarming enemies, and increasing space. Their bullets were striking intervening objects, and the range was too far for the deadly revolvers with which they excelled.

"Run, Saber, if yuh ever run before!" muttered Bob Pryor, glancing back over his shoulder at the gathering human storm.

Quantrell was leaping around in his fury

at the escape of the Federal agent. Thompson had run over and joined Quantrell, was telling him just who the Rio Kid was — a Federal officer, a bloodhound who had been commissioned to hunt down the guerrillas. Thompson had seen him at the H Bar, and had no doubt made inquiries and spied on him, checking him.

There had been no time for the Rio Kid to choose directions. He had seized the quickest, most hopeful line of escape, seeking only to get a few yards between himself and Quantrell's guns. He was flashing south now, on a wood trail, the dun picking the easiest underfooting. A slip of a hoof, an unseen stone or a rotten bit of ground, and it would be over for the Rio Kid.

But the dun did not slip. Sure-footed as a mountain burro, rested, and unafraid of gunfire and singing lead, Saber carried his master and friend out of the terrible death-trap.

The wind whined in the Rio Kid's ears as he galloped on south, taking a winding way that led on and on through broken country. Now and then, as he cocked his ear, he heard a shot or a hoarse shout from behind, and knew they were coming. He was not yet safe.

Quantrell would be furious, wild with

seething rage, and so would the giant Thompson, his comrade in crime. Together they had planned death for Haven's people in Kansas. Thompson's fiendish desire for profit, wanting to take the ranchers' lands, would be put into deeds by Quantrell unless something happened to stop them — and soon.

"I got to warn them Kansas folks about that and see they're pertected," he thought anxiously. "But first we must run clear, Saber."

Quantrell, Todd, Cole and Jim Younger, and Jesse and Frank James — such fellows would cling to a trail with bulldog ferocity. They would thirst for his blood, and never let up. They were all first-class horsemen as well as sharpshooters, and it would not be an easy matter to shake them off.

He hit some meadows, open spaces half a mile across. Glancing back as he made for some dark pine woods on the other side, he saw the van of the pursuit that was settling down to a long run, break from the chaparral where he had been a few minutes ago. They set up a blood-curdling yowl, the Rebel yell, as they sighted him, and some tried for him with revolvers. But the range was long. Then the dun picked out an opening and dashed through a woods trail, the

Rio Kid keeping low to avoid being swept off by overhanging branches of trees.

He wanted to swing around, get on a road that would take him northwest, for Kansas, but his pursuers were spread out and the contour of the country made this impossible. He was driven on and on southward, cursing the ill-luck that had betrayed him to Quantrell.

With chagrin he realized that Fate had played him a cruel trick by bringing Thompson to Quantrell's camp, at the time he was there. He had been close to making the connection he had needed to place the guerrillas within Terrell's range so that they could be captured.

On the other hand, he knew he was fortunate to have escaped from Quantrell's camp with his neck. Not many men had done so, once in his grip.

All he could do now was to ride like a mad centaur, try to shake off the guerrilla band and eventually hope to swing and head for Kansas. . . .

It was days later, when the Rio Kid, riding and circling, being forced southward, but finally managing to outmaneuver his pursuing foes, that Lieutenant Martin Grew rode up to the H Bar. He eagerly looked for Edith Haven, for she had been in his mind and heart, and the thought of again seeing her thrilled him.

A week had passed since he had seen her, and he was hungry for sight of her. He had been unable, since meeting her and being drawn to her more closely through the experiences they had shared than otherwise would have been possible, to get her out of his thoughts. He did not want to. He was in love with Edith and meant to ask her to marry him.

The news from the Potomac was getting better and better. It was safe to say that victory was now in sight for the Union forces. Grant had been driving on, steam-roller fashion, against the gallant but tired and ill-equipped divisions of the great Southern leader, General Robert E. Lee. Lee was a wonderful general, a military genius, but the blockade had cut off all supplies save trickles that did little to keep the Confederate armies in the field.

It looked as if the War would soon be over, and when it was, Grew hoped to marry Edith Haven and settle down on his ranch in Kansas. The prospect was heavenly to him after the long, terrible years of the War between men who were brothers.

Dismounting, Grew watered his horse lightly and, unsaddling, turned the animal into a corral. He had been busy at his task, hunting cavalry mounts for the Army, and was on his way back to Lawrence.

Swinging around to the shady side of the house, he stopped abruptly. The big Major Jarvis Thompson was sitting on a bench beside George Haven, talking with him earnestly.

"Why not sell — yuh can't go on without money, Haven," Grew heard Thompson say.

"Well — mebbe I will . . . Oh, howdy, Lieutenant! Yuh're a sight for sore eyes! Oh, Edie! He's back!"

Edith hurried from the kitchen lean-to which was again usable, for much of the fire damage had been repaired. Her violet eyes came alive with joy as she saw Grew. Smiling, she put out her hand to him.

Grew laughed as he took her hand, greeting her.

Then he became aware that Major Thompson was glowering at him. He swung, and saluted.

"Good afternoon, Major. Warm today."

He noted that Thompson's face had been scratched and cut. It seemed to have been spattered with tiny, hard bits of something, lead or rock.

"Hullo, Grew," Thompson growled.

From the start, Grew had not cared very

106

much for the big fellow. It had not been a strong enough emotion to rouse suspicion in him, but he had known a slight, jarring feeling whenever he had come in contact with Thompson. He had ascribed it to some natural and not unusual antagonism in personalities between two men who meet by chance.

"The major's askin' me to sell out here, Lieutenant," remarked Haven. He looked into Grew's face, earnestly, adding, "I thought I better."

"Mr. Haven," said Grew, "I told you when I was here before that I'd be glad to help you. I meant it then and I mean it now. I don't like to interfere in your deal, Major Thompson, but I honestly believe Mr. Haven would be foolish to dump his ranch at a low price now. The war will soon be over and peace on the land. Business will recover and beef ought to form a big market for those ready to take advantage of it. I'm thinking of going in for it myself."

Thompson's face turned a shade redder. He bit at his mustache.

" 'Pears to me, Lieutenant," he said harshly, "that yuh've got a nose for everybody's business but yore own! I've seldom come here that I haven't tripped over yuh. I wonder what yore superiors would say if

107

they knew yuh spend most of yore time hanging around a pretty girl!"

Grew felt his face flush hot and crimson. He tried to control himself, but found it difficult to brook the insults Thompson flung at him. Had it not been for his strict military training he would have punched Thompson's words back with a fist.

"Beg your pardon, Major Thompson," he replied, as evenly as he could. "This is not an official matter but a personal one." Turning to Haven, he ignored the fuming Thompson. "I want to make you a loan, Mr. Haven," he said. "I'll be happy to help your friends out, too, as far as I'm able. I have a good deal of pay coming to me and money from my parents, and it's yours and your friends' as long as it lasts. You can at least buy some provisions and seed, and a few head of breed cattle to improve the wild longhorns you can capture."

"I think that's wonderful of you!" Edith cried.

"It is — mighty white of yuh, Lieutenant," Haven said gratefully.

The rancher and his pretty daughter had been greatly shocked by Thompson's rudeness to their friend. They were on Grew's side, and the big man realized he had made an error, as Haven drawled:

"Major, I ain't sellin'. Not yet, anyways. I'm acceptin' the lieutenant's offer of help — a grub-stake we'll call it. I'll pay it back, Martin."

Major Thompson, who appeared to Grew to be greatly shaken, tried to back up and undo the harm he had caused by his sneering words.

"Very well, Haven — all right, Lieutenant. Sorry I spoke that way."

"Don't mention it," Grew said coolly.

He held out his arm to Edith, and the two strolled off together.

"Have you heard anything from Captain Pryor?" Edith asked Lieutenant Grew.

He shook his head. "No. I'd hoped you folks might have . . . How long have you known Major Thompson, Edith?"

"Oh, we knew him slightly before the War. He lived in Missouri but came to Kansas and was in the feed business in Lawrence. Father met him, and lately he's started to call on us a lot. I don't like him very much. Do you?"

"I hadn't thought much about it before, but I don't."

The antagonism he had sensed had flared into strong dislike, after Thompson's angry insults. And with this came suspicion.

"Queer way for an officer to behave," he

thought.

Then he decided that he would check up on Thompson. A wire to the War Department would do the trick.

CHAPTER X
CLOSE CALL

Major Thompson, to everybody's relief, did not stay long. He rode off toward Lawrence after a time. Grew remained for supper, but since he also wished to be in Lawrence in the morning, he took his leave about eight o'clock.

He was saddling up when he turned to find Edith close to him.

"Good-by, Lieutenant," she murmured.

The strength of his feeling for the girl overcame him at that moment. Seizing her in his arms he kissed her.

"I love you, Edith!" he whispered eagerly. "I want you to marry me! Will you?"

"Yes, Martin — yes!" she whispered back, her blue eyes shining. "And, oh, I'm so happy — so happy!"

She laughed with sheer joy. Ahead, the two of them could see a rosy life. They were young, and so trouble and care were easily shed.

When Grew left her he, too, felt happy —
and for the first time since the war had
begun. Riding toward Lawrence in the
night, he found himself whistling.

The constant, wearing wind over the rolling lands did not bother him especially. It
was always present, but he had been born
to it. Sometimes people who tried to settle
there couldn't stand the wind, which flung
grit and dust into the interstices of homes,
clothing and into the eyes and nostrils.

There was a slice of moon, and the stars
were bright. Bits of fluff sent little shadows
scudding over the short grass. Grew was
thinking of Edith, but more somber
thoughts were also in his mind — thoughts
of Major Thompson.

"I'll telegraph the War Department on
Thompson in the morning," he decided.
"It's mighty strange the way he acts. Deter-
mined to get the H Bar —"

There were other things Grew intended to
do in town the next day also. For he meant
to make arrangements to transfer funds to
the bank there, for the use of George Haven
and his rancher friends. He had several
thousand dollars and, judiciously used, that
sum might serve to eke out the resources of
the settlers until business affairs were better.

Absorbed in his thoughts of Edith and her people, Grew was startled to attention as his gray gelding suddenly shied and sniffed. He was passing an ebony-dark patch of cottonwoods that loomed on his right as the trail to town ran near a stream.

"Quiet, boy — quiet," murmured Grew.

The wind rattled the brush, but then there was a heavy noise just behind him, and Grew swung in his saddle to see the black bulk of a rider driving from the woods upon him. The man had evidently been hidden there, waiting for him.

Something metallic caught the silver rays of the moon. It was, Grew saw, a revolver, aimed at his heart.

"Yuh young skunk!" snarled a hard voice. "Did yuh think I'd let yuh get away with that? Suspicious now, too, ain't yuh? Goin' to check up on me."

It was Major Jarvis Thompson.

Martin Grew knew too much about firearms to make a move under Thompson's steady gun. The man was not more than two yards from him, and the dripping hate in his voice told Grew he would be glad to pull the trigger.

In fact, Grew had but one slight hope, and that was that Thompson had not yet fired. He was too busy talking, cursing Grew.

Perhaps he had to lash himself to killing fury. Or he may have been the sort of man who had to let his victim know who finished him. Anyhow, he was gloating over the lieutenant, rubbing it in.

Grew's only chance was to keep Thompson talking, and watch for the faintest opportunity to put up a fight.

"Why, Major," he exclaimed, "what are you talking about? If you're angry because I promised to lend Haven money, why, I won't do it. Why should I think you needed to be checked up on?"

As he talked, saying whatever came quickly to his mind, Grew eased the gray around with a slight pressure of his knee so that he was facing Thompson.

"Stand, curse yuh, or I'll blow yuh to Kingdom Come!" roared Thompson.

He was at murder pitch, and had let his intended victim know who was sending the lead into his vitals. The man's teeth gleamed as he snarled, and Grew realized that he was going to die in an instant.

Grew was a fighting man. He had faced enemy lead with cool nerve on the battlefield. He did not intend to go down now without at least a show of resistance, and he flung himself violently from the saddle, straight toward Thompson. The big fellow's

114

Colt roared, dazing him, singeing his cheek, and he felt the agonizing smash of a big slug through the flesh of his upper left arm.

Thompson's ghost-colored stallion bucked at the explosion, and the major's follow-up shot missed by inches. Grew had hold of the big man's thick, strong gun-wrist, and the lieutenant's weight, with the sudden jerk of the powerful stallion, twisted Thompson from his seat.

He fell as Grew held on for his life, the blood roaring in his ears. In the terrific excitement of the hand-to-hand combat, Grew overcame the shock and pain of his injury.

It was man to man. Thompson outweighed Grew by nearly a hundred pounds, and while ordinarily Grew's youth and nerve would have evened that somewhat, the wound he had received was already weakening him.

They hit the ground hard, and Thompson, unable to use his revolver as Grew kept his grip on his wrist, brought up a knee and rammed it into the tall young soldier's belly. Locked in furious embrace, smashing at one another as best they could, they strained for the advantage. Thompson's chief idea was to turn the big Colt in his right hand so the muzzle would be against Grew's body, while

Grew had to keep it off.

Using an old wrestling trick, Grew suddenly gave way and changed the direction of his power. Thompson was thrown half off, and slewed around. There was a cracking sound as the major's own weight strained his gun elbow and, with a yelp of pain, Thompson dropped his pistol.

But even as Grew won this point, it changed Thompson's tactics. The big man concentrated on beating Grew senseless, and his physical advantages of weight began to tell. He smashed his great fists into Grew's face and stomach, swearing in his rage.

Grew kicked at him, punched back, tearing at Thompson's eyes with his quick hands. He made several hits that jarred the attacker. Thompson came up on his knees and threw himself on the young soldier, and his strong fingers found Grew's throat.

Struggle as he would, with Thompson's whole weight on him, Grew could not break the grip. Lights danced before his eyes, and he knew that within a minute he would be throttled, and finished off at Thompson's leisure.

Suddenly he found he could breathe again; with a final effort, he shifted, and as his senses cleared somewhat, he saw that

Thompson had left him and was leaping on his horse.

He could not understand this. Why had the big man, at the point of victory, decided to let him live? Then he caught the glint of another gun, which Thompson had drawn from inside his tunic, a weapon carried in a shoulder-holster.

As Thompson swung the stallion, he threw his spare pistol up and fired once, twice, at Grew. But the lieutenant had twitched aside, flipping into the dark brush. He heard the bullets plug into the ground, and grit spattered him, but he was not again hit.

Thompson dug in his spurs and went galloping away, and Grew, getting out his own pistol, sent three shots after him.

For several minutes he lay where he was, trying to pull himself together. The wind still blew, rustling the sered leaves. The sound of Thompson's horse had died away, northeastward, and as Grew, his breast heaving, and the pain coming into his wounded arm, listened with hyper-sensitive ears, he could hear nothing more than the sounds Nature made.

The puzzle as to why Thompson had quit just at the moment of victory, when Grew would have been unconscious and easily disposed of, was one Grew could not then solve. He could only lie there, waiting for strength to come back into his limbs.

Minutes passed, but they dragged interminably. At last Grew, with the blood oozing slowly from his lacerated left upper arm, felt he could rise. His horse had run off some yards, and had dropped its head to graze on a patch of clump grass.

The lieutenant got to his knees, gripping the limb of a thick bush close at hand. The rustling noises he made sounded loud in the night. Then a voice said, almost in his ear:

"Freeze and throw up yore hands!"

A cocking gun told Grew he was covered from the back. Someone had come across the creek, afoot, and had crept up on him like an Indian, without the slightest warning noise.

"Who's that?" growled Grew. "Don't shoot."

"The main question is," the voice replied, "who are you and what's the gunplay mean?"

Grew figured it out swiftly. Thompson must have heard the hoofs of the horse ridden by this man, whoever he was, while Thompson had been choking him. Alarmed, the major had run away. That being the case, then this man might be a friend. Grew decided to chance it.

"I'm Lieutenant Grew," he said. "I was just set upon by a killer, and I'm wounded."

"Grew! Hold yore fire, now! This is the Rio Kid — Cap'n Pryor."

A moment later, the lithe figure of the Rio Kid crouched at Grew's side.

"I heard some shots, and veered over — was on my way to the H Bar and then Lawrence," Pryor said. "What was it all about, Lieutenant?"

"Thompson — Major Thompson — was lyin' in wait for me here," gasped Grew, gripping his friend's hand. "I don't savvy what it was about, altogether, though he was angry because I offered to help Haven out and I told Haven not to sell at a song to Thompson. That was this afternoon. Thompson acted so queer that I decided I'd wire Washington and check up on him. I began to wonder if he was really a U.S. officer."

"Yuh're hurt, ain't yuh? How bad?"

"Just — just a drill through the flesh, upper left arm. I'll be all right in a minute."

"Thompson rode off?"

"Yes, some time ago, when he heard your horse."

"Huh! I was ridin' in an awful rush."

"I'd like a smoke," Grew remarked. "It'd

buck me up. Reckon it's safe to light up here?"

"I reckon so. We'll chance it. I need one myself."

CHAPTER XI
ATTACK!

Bob Pryor, the Rio Kid, swiftly rolled two quirlies, and passed one to Grew. He struck a match, which sizzled, and then the waxed stick took fire, shaded in Pryor's hand.

As Grew drew in on his cigarette, the light showed the bewhiskered, blood-stained face of the Rio Kid, his torn clothing and bandit get-up. Deep lines of fatigue were under his eyes, racked with the agony of keeping awake for the days and nights he had had no sleep at all.

"Good heavens, Cap'n!" exclaimed Grew. "You're worse off than I am!"

"Scratches, that's all," muttered Pryor, squatted on his haunches and enjoying the cigarette. "I been ridin' sixty hours without a break save to rest the dun and grab a drink of water. Quantrell and his whole gang was on my trail and they run me south of fifty miles, 'fore I managed to back track in a creek and shake 'em off. Thompson beat me up here easy enough, since Quantrell had me runnin'."

"Thompson! You mean the man who attacked me?"

"Sure. He's no Union officer, Grew. He's a spy for Quantrell, one of the band of guerrillas. That uniform he wears is a masquerade and he's got no right to it."

"So that's it! Everything's clearer now. Why, Thompson was around the day before Quantrell hit Haven and run off those horses!"

The Rio Kid nodded, the cigarette glowing red as he inhaled.

"Reckon Thompson give Quantrell the tip off when to grab 'em. Them hosses made the Lawrence raid possible. Cuss Thompson! He rode into Quantrell's bivouac in Missouri and reckernized me. That's why I've had such a tough run of it, and just when I hoped to snare Quantrell and his whole gang."

The Rio Kid straightened up.

"Quantrell's attackin' Haven again, and the line of ranches, at Thompson's order, Grew," he said grimly. "That's why I've got to warn 'em, pronto, why I aimed for here first. I've got to get in touch with Cap'n Terrell, too, as soon as possible. Mebbe he can rush some cavalry over here in time to beat off Quantrell when he comes."

"When will Quantrell strike?"

"I ain't shore, but if he does it at all, it'll be pronto. They don't savvy where I am, but they'll figger they can beat me to it. I don't s'pose Thompson knew who I was tonight, did he?"

"I don't see how he could have. He lost his nerve when he heard someone comin', that's all."

The Rio Kid, by the light of matches, managed to put a rough bandage on Grew's wound.

"How yuh feel, Lieutenant?" he asked then. "Strong enough to ride?"

Grew nodded. The narrow escape he had had he threw off. His shoulder throbbed, but his youthful strength held him up. Shock in such men did not last long and could be overcome, whereas in an older person it might prove fatal.

"I can ride, Captain," he said firmly.

"*Bueno* — good. There's two things to be done. One, warn Haven and his friends, second, ride to Lawrence and call Terrell."

Grew understood that the Rio Kid was giving him his choice.

"I can make Lawrence if you want me to," the lieutenant said.

"Fine! My hoss is done in, and the Haven

ranch is only a few miles more. Lawrence is a lot farther. Besides, I want to be on hand in case Quantrell comes."

"Take care of her — of them all!"

"I'll guarantee she ain't hurt," the Rio Kid promised. He guessed that Grew was worried about Edith Haven.

"Your message to Captain Terrell?" asked Grew.

"Tell him I believe Quantrell will attack here, mebbe within hours, and to rush out as many men as he can at once. I'll collect 'em at Haven's."

"Right."

Grew rose. He felt shaky, but could walk. The Rio Kid gave a whistle, and a dun horse, Saber, came walking up. The dun was covered with mud and dust, and his usually sleek hide was scratched by thorns.

Pryor patted Saber's neck, spoke to him as he hit leather. He caught Grew's horse, and helped the lieutenant mount. Gripping hands, the two young men parted, Grew heading straight for Lawrence, while Captain Pryor, the Rio Kid, made for Haven's H Bar Ranch.

Quantrell was coming, somewhere out there in the black night, Quantrell, the killer, to strike with all his mad fury.

As the Rio Kid rode off toward the Haven

ranch, he knew that he must have sleep and hot food, and that the dun was in even worse need of rest.

Saber had successfully outrun the swift horses of Quantrell's command, but it had taken everything the animal and his master had to make their escape. The run to Kansas had been harrowing. The Rio Kid dared not let down, for he knew Quantrell's caliber. He had headed direct over the rolling, wooded land, onto the Kansas plains, toward the H Bar.

Half an hour after parting from Lieutenant Martin Grew, the Rio Kid pushed the tired dun into Haven's yard and dismounted by the light of the moon. Taking off the sweated saddle and bridle, and rubbing Saber down, he turned the horse into the grassy grazing corral at the back of the barn.

Then, wearily, all but walking in his sleep, with his eyelids unable to stay open, he staggered to Haven's door.

The place was dark. It was late, and such people retired early. He banged on the portal, however, calling out who he was so that Haven would hear and know it was a friend.

"All right — I'm comin'," Haven's sleepy voice answered at last.

The bar was lifted, and Haven opened the door.

"C'mon in, Cap'n — glad to see yuh. What's up?"

"Trouble," the Rio Kid told him quickly. "Quantrell's aimed yore way again, Haven. Yuh'll have to call in all yore friends, and make it pronto. Fetch 'em all here, women and kids, and their guns and ammunition, and we'll try to hold the guerrillas off till help comes. I met Grew back a ways and he's givin' the alarm in Lawrence."

"Curse Quantrell! Seems to me he's loco. What can he want with us? We ain't got anything left, after that raid he made on our hosses!"

"Yuh got land — and Quantrell's workin' with Jarvis Thompson, supposed to be a friend of yores. You know, the one in the major's uniform. He set on Martin Grew tonight and near killed him. He's a spy and a guerrilla."

"Thompson!" exclaimed Haven.

"Is — is Martin hurt?"

The Rio Kid turned, to see the anxious, white face of Edith Haven peering from her doorway.

"He got a cut, but he's all right, ma'am. He'll be here tomorrow, so don't you worry."

Haven lit a candle. As the yellow flame came up he, as had Grew, gaped with astonishment at the aspect of the Rio Kid.

"By glory, I'd never have knowed yuh, Cap'n! Yuh looked drawed through a key-hole and a muddy one at that!"

"I've had a tough ride. Got to rest, Haven, and now. Warn yore friends — Quantrell's comin' — start right away, savvy? No time — no time —"

The warmth of the cabin, the relaxation of having at last reached his goal, suddenly overcame the Rio Kid.

"Come to my bunk, and —" began Haven, but the man before him had sunk to the floor and was sleeping.

Haven picked him up, carried him over and laid him on the bed. He covered the Rio Kid with a blanket and, pulling on his own pants and jacket, strapped his gun-belt on.

"Watch over him, Edie," he admonished. "I'll be back pronto. I'll ride to Milt Young's and he can take it up from there. I'll come home soon as I've started Milt off."

The Rio Kid woke with a start. The rectangular patches marking the narrow, loophole windows of the rancher's cabin were a faint gray, marking the early dawn. But the wind was shrieking with a high-pitched, fanatic note, and spattering rain-drops were falling on the slanting roof.

His great physical endurance and training had enabled him to drive through without sleep. And now, after a few hours of rest, Bob Pryor could rise and take up where he had left off.

George Haven sat in the rear of the room, quietly cleaning a rifle and putting cartridges for it into the loops of a belt. Edith was out in the kitchen, starting a fire with which to cook hot coffee and breakfast for the expected guests, the people of the ranches who had been notified to hurry to the H Bar for their defense.

Mrs. Milt Young, a stout, capable woman with graying hair, and a girl in her 'teens, Sally Young, were helping Edith. They had come at once to the Haven ranch, while Young rode with the warning to the other ranches.

A shout from down the slope sent Pryor to the door; he glanced out, and saw the Schultzes coming in a spring wagon, the whole family together.

The rain had not yet begun falling hard, but came in big drops that splashed with great force against the buildings. The Rio Kid borrowed a towel and went out to the pump. He had been riding without shaving

128

or the chance to clean up and he spent half an hour at this, during which time the Phillips brothers arrived with their wives and small children. On their heels came a group of twenty women, children and men, the latter heavily armed with pistols, shotguns and rifles, and belts of bullets for them.

After cleaning up, mending his clothing as best he could, and putting on a fresh shirt that he carried in his saddlebag, the Rio Kid watched the southeast anxiously. From time to time he would turn and hunt with his keen eyes toward Lawrence.

Quantrell should come one way, and the hoped for reinforcements which Lieutenant Grew was supposed to summon, should come from the other.

The light was poor, for the gray clouds made the sky leaden and the sun, rising behind them, did not show although the visibility grew a little better after an hour. It was only six A.M.

The breakfast was ready and everybody, except a man who stood guard out past the barn, sat down to the meal, most of them squatting on the floor as there were not enough chairs to go around. The ranchhouse was crowded with women and children, with the waiting fighters, Haven's friends.

129

The hot food braced the Rio Kid tremendously, after his sleep. He felt himself again, after the ordeal through which he had gone.

Some rode up, calling out. It was Milt Young, who had carried the warning to the farthest of the ranches. Now all were at Haven's, and the men, with some thirty guns, were ready for action.

The clouds opened up and rain poured down on the roof, sweeping in sheets across the plains. There were few breaks to check the force of the storm and the visibility became almost zero as water raged from the sky.

The noise of the storm roared in the Rio Kid's ears. Would Quantrell attack at such a time?

"I don't reckon them guerrillas'll be out in this," someone said loudly.

"Sh-h!" cried Haven. "What's that?"

The faintly recognizable crack of a rifle, followed by two more shots, came to them. Their sentry, at the barn, ran full-tilt, head down to the storm, across the yard.

The Rio Kid held the door open for him, braced against the wind that sought to tear it from its hinges. The drenched guard, Ed Garvey, a rancher of fifty whose family was safe in the group shouted:

"Here they come! It's Quantrell!"

"Bar the doors!" roared the Rio Kid, snatching out a Colt and pulling back the hammer spur under his thumb. "Take yore loopholes, boys!"

They were quickly ready for defense. Peeping from one side of a window, the Rio Kid saw a mass of hard-riding devils in ponchos, and with Stetsons strapped low as they headed into the violent wind, loom up near the big barn.

"Hold yore fire till they're in," he cautioned. "Ready, now!"

CHAPTER XII
DEFENDERS

It was difficult to estimate the exact number of the attackers in the whipping, blinding rainstorm. They were coming around both sides of the barn now, in small bunches of twos and threes, and heading straight at the house.

Probably Quantrell and Thompson figured the occupants would be totally off guard in such weather. Anyhow they were forced to strike, quickly, if they wished to win, for the escape of the Rio Kid made this imperative.

"Sixty — seventy — must be a hunderd or more," decided Pryor, letting them rush to within fifty yards of the house.

"Now!" he cried, and lifted the thumb off his pistol hammer.

He knew he had made a hit, as his heavy pistol roared, for a guerrilla in the van — he was on a chestnut horse but the Rio Kid could not recognize him because of the Stetson brim and the enveloping poncho —

threw up his arms and crashed from his saddle. The killer lay in the pool of rainwater as he landed, and crushing hoofs from following mustangs hit his body.

A breath later, and the thirty ranchers and their cowboys and friends let go. They did not shoot all together but close, the explosions joining as each man took his deliberate aim and pulled trigger.

Four guerrillas, taken by the point-blank fire, were knocked from their horses, while others could be seen to wince or show signs of having been hit by the Kansas lead.

The roaring guns crashed, deafening all inside the ranchhouse. But its effect was tremendous on the Quantrell men, who had not expected such a greeting. Horses reared high, their hoofs sliding in the muddy, wet yard as they sought to turn.

"Fire! Let 'em have it!"

A wild, infuriated man on a ghost-gray stallion, a huge fellow, shrieked and roared the commands over the bellowing storm. He discharged his revolvers at the windows, over and over again, while the cool-headed guerrillas, pulling themselves together, shot with both hands, using their Colts skillfully and hanging on with their steel-muscled knees.

The bullets from the attackers drove like

hail through the narrow windows. Some ripped through the panels of the door, but the walls stopped the lead.

Three men were hit inside. They collapsed quietly, under their window gaps, while others leaped to take their places and women hurried over with basins of warm water and clean cloths to tend the wounded.

"Keep to the side on those volleys — don't show yoreselves," warned the Rio Kid. "Bob up to shoot!"

His snarling Colt hunted for the big fellow he thought must be Major Jarvis Thompson. In the driving rain, with the riders keeping their heads down and the ponchos concealing their shoulders and trunks, it was hard to identify individuals.

"They're all in there, Quantrell!" bellowed the huge horseman.

Then he felt the wind of Pryor's slugs, and one cut him across the face. He glanced up, toward the house, and the Rio Kid glimpsed the twisted, angry features of Thompson.

The charge brought them dangerously close to the house. One bold guerrilla slid up to the front door and began smashing at the wood with his carbine butt. The Rio Kid could not see him from the window, the angle being too great.

"Fire, boys!" he shouted, and bounded to the splintering portal. "Drive 'em back, now or never!"

A board smashed in from the heavy blows of the rifle butt, and daylight showed. The Rio Kid, crouched to one side, teeth showing as he fought threw bullets into the wood, aware that they would pass on through. Suddenly the beating on the door ceased.

Jumping back to his window opening, he saw that two more guerrillas lay silent in the yard. Then he glimpsed Quantrell, up at the other end of the house, shouting orders to his men.

He raised his revolver to draw a bead on the guerrilla chief, but Quantrell seemed to have the devil's own luck and bear a charmed life. For suddenly he jerked his horse around, shifting just as Pryor let go at him. Quantrell had passed safely through the most perilous situations, again and again, often without a scratch.

Evidently Quantrell had ordered his men back, for the guerrillas yanked reins and veered, riding out into a wide circle about the house and pouring their bullets in from this Indian formation. They yelled as they moved, shooting from the flank at the windows.

"Save yore ammunition and let 'em waste theirs," commanded the Rio Kid.

He breathed a sigh of relief as he saw the guerrillas beaten off in their first mad rush. He needed time, time for Grew and Terrell to get in from Lawrence.

Picking up a carbine, he went to a loophole and peeked out. A bullet from a revolver shrieked through, almost striking his skull, but he threw the carbine to shoulder and pulled trigger. The guerrilla at whom he had aimed was moving fast. His horse leaped in the air and the man flew from his back, landing on his belly in the mud.

The attackers drew farther off at this exhibition of marksmanship, and the Rio Kid, carefully observing them, saw they were having a council of war. Quantrell, the huge Thompson, and other figures he could not identify, were huddled together in the wind and rain with their heads close.

"They won't have much luck burnin' us out today," he thought grimly. "That's their favorite game."

But since the rain had wet the wood of the house Quantrell would not be able to set it afire easily this time.

Then the guerrillas, who evidently had reasoned out the true state of affairs, that most of their prey were in the Haven home and on guard, rode a wide circle around to the barn, coming up behind it. They dismounted, leaving their horses on the far side, and began entering the large structure. Soon, gunfire opened up once more on the house, concentrated on the windows.

"They're stayin'," Pryor thought uneasily.

He ordered the women and children to keep down behind the barrier of furniture in the main room, and most of his men to the side of the house facing the barn. They could not see their foes now, but the bullets steadily zipped through the loopholes, the guerrillas displaying their usual brand of ace marksmanship.

"They're goin' to wait till dark falls," Haven suggested, squatted down by the Rio Kid. "Then they'll rush the house."

"Grew'll be back 'fore that," Pryor replied.

At least, so he hoped. But as an hour and then another went by, and no sign of reinforcements came, he began to wonder what could have befallen Lieutenant Martin Grew. Had he run afoul of Thompson again on his way to Lawrence? Had his horse thrown him, because in his weakened condition Grew had been unable to keep on?

It was after noon, and still Quantrell and his devilish crew held the barn, and the ranchers in the house must stay put. To venture out into such fire as these men holed-up in the barn could put up would mean death, or at least serious wounds.

The terrific storm had blown over. Gray, leaden clouds still raced across the sky, but the wind was drying off the wood of the house walls. The pools had disappeared from the yard, drained into the earth.

If night came, thought the Rio Kid, there would be an awful shambles. The guerrillas could creep up to the walls and batter through, get in among them, slaughter them all.

Where, he thought over and over, was Lieutenant Grew? Why didn't he come?

Lieutenant Grew, could he have but known it, had done his best. Especially in view of the fact that he had known that Edith Haven might be in dire danger. But he had encountered unexpected difficulties on his mission to the town of Lawrence.

In spite of the terrific duel he had fought with the giant Jarvis Thompson, and the shock and loss of blood from the wound, Martin Grew had reached Lawrence in good time. It was late and the town, for the most part, was darkened.

Grew pushed his weary horse to Terrell's headquarters, a square wooden frame house on Main Street of the town. There was a sentry on guard who challenged him, and he identified himself.

"Sir, Cap'n Terrell ain't here," the guard informed him, after presenting arms in salute. "The troops done rode out an hour ago."

Grew swore inwardly, nodded, and went inside. A second lieutenant came from Terrell's office and they exchanged salutes.

"Captain Terrell received an emergency alarm, Lieutenant Grew," the young officer told him. "Major Thompson brought him information concerning the guerrilla chief, Quantrell. He said that Quantrell was sleeping at a farmhouse only fifteen miles southeast of town."

"Thompson!" muttered Grew. "Curse him!"

He understood the game at once. Thompson had beaten him in, and had given the false alarm which had sent Terrell and most of the seasoned cavalry out of Lawrence.

He had the officer in charge send a messenger on Terrell's trail, then sought to find mounted fighting men with whom to hurry to the H Bar. This was not easy, for everybody wanted to capture Quantrell, on whose head rested large rewards, besides the glory that would fall to the lot of his conqueror.

Terrell's crack cavalry, routed out in a hurry, during the night, had told watching eyes what must be up. So many citizen posses had been quickly formed and had saddled up to trail the soldiers in the hope of getting in on the kill.

Martin Grew, sweating with his knowledge of what would happen if Quantrell's terrible killers hit Haven's place, sought trained fighters that he could lead back to the battle.

The second lieutenant supplied him with his best chance. He informed Grew that there was a troop of state militia, mounted, camped about ten miles the other side of Lawrence, on the river. After telling the officer to round up as many men as possible, Grew changed horses and galloped out to the encampment.

Here he had to identify himself, waken the colonel commanding the militia, and then convince the officer of the need for hurry.

At last, riding alongside the militia leader, Grew got started with sixty armed and mounted men, toward the H Bar. But the gray of dawn was already showing over the plains as they swung into a trot. With such a band the faster horses were always held down to the pace of the slowest. The colonel refused to push the animals hard at the outset, too, since they must be carefully warmed up.

Then the wind hit them, the rising gale bringing the rain. It was in their faces and it slowed them. Pausing only to don their ponchos, the troopers pushed on, heads down to the shrieking wind, which smote them with all its fury. The downpour began and the prairie became a sheet of water, the horses sinking to the hocks, and the pace became maddeningly slow.

Grew would have ridden on ahead, but dared not leave the militia. He feared the colonel might decide to lie up until the storm blew over.

They seemed, to the frantic Grew, who had a difficult time hiding his emotion, to move at snail's pace, against the violent gale and stinging rain. It was a walk, now, in the sticky mud. Ammunition had to be kept dry and the carbine barrels protected. These were unseasoned troops, older men and boys, from Kansas, and could not be hurried.

CHAPTER XIII
ON THE FLANK

For about an hour the rain had been falling when the troops with Lieutenant Grew came to a little rill over which, on his way in the night before, Grew had sent his horse leaping across in a single bound. Now it was roaring along like a mountain torrent. It was fifty yards wide, and spread out in the shallow depression through which it ran. It took half an hour to cross the stream.

With this warning in view, Grew was not surprised when, on reaching the creek which had to be forded in order to get over on the H Bar range, they found it was as wide as a big river, and that it had flooded the plain for half a mile. In the center rushed a mad current, fighting itself, thick with dark silt, almost black in the leaden light. Sticks and debris were carried along on the white-capped heart of the stream.

"We'll never cross that!" the colonel shouted to Grew over the roar of the water and the shrieking wind.

They were all drenched, in spite of the protective capes. The wind drove the moisture through to their skins.

Evidently the rain had fallen heavily above, and even before the storm had struck the locality the streams had started to rise.

Grew cursed and pushed his horse into the flood. The militia, hunched drearily over their mounts, watched him as he drove his mustang into the creek. Soon the animal lost footing and began swimming, carried down by the current as it took him. Grew sought to urge him across but big floating logs hit the horse and turned him back.

Finally Grew, some hundreds of yards down, came out on the same bank and rode wearily back to the troopers.

"Let's try higher up," suggested the colonel.

They rode northwest along the eastern bank of the erstwhile creek, seeking a way over. It was noon before they managed to get across the raging waters. The storm had blown on by then, and already the current was diminishing.

Well around on the north of the H Bar, Grew swung the militia south on the flooded, wet plain. The hoofs of the horses sank deep, making sucking noises as they moved. Mile by mile they drew closer to the ranch, where Grew hoped all was well. Perhaps Quantrell had not yet struck.

The whole prairie looked black, and the mud was as black as ink. Straining his eyes and ears, for the wind was still blowing hard, Grew thought he heard some distant gunshots, but the visibility was poor and it was difficult to hear.

Doggedly they shoved along. Suddenly the colonel roared:

"Here they come! Get ready, men!"

It was about three-thirty in the afternoon. The trip had taken three times as long as it should have under normal conditions.

Grew pulled his reins, staring toward the H Bar from the slight rise they had just breasted. He could see the low house and barn standing up from the plains. And over the rise appeared a line of sixty mounted guerrillas, spread out over the flat, and bearing straight down upon them!

"Quantrell!" somebody yelled.

A shudder of apprehension went through the green troopers. Quantrell had massacred more than one Federal band sent to take him. But they stood well. However, they were bunching up, closing ranks.

"Tell 'em to spread out — hold their fire!" Grew begged the leader.

But the colonel had his own ideas of military tactics. His bugler trilled squadron formation and the men wheeled into a ragged column of fours and waited for the charge.

The wild guerrillas came pounding on. They carried big Colt .45s in their hands, but they did not shoot. An excited trooper fired his carbine without the command, and half of his companions followed suit.

"Hold that!" bellowed the colonel. "Wait till they're in!"

The earth shook with the beating of hoofs as Quantrell's men raged down on the militia. Fierce bearded faces loomed up, each guerrilla a powerful fighting unit and able to kill from a full gallop. They would not waste any lead. They held in their fire until they were within a few paces of the soldiers.

Carbines began cracking all along the column of massed troopers. The colonel, as brave as a lion, was out in front, saber drawn.

"Come on, boys!" he yelled, and dug in his spurs.

Quantrell showed in the center of the on-riding guerrillas, with Jesse James and Cole Younger flanking him. Cool as ice, the guerrillas ripped in, and suddenly the shrill

Rebel yell curdled the blood of the unseasoned soldiers.

Quantrell, James and Younger were within two yards of the colonel when their revolvers bellowed, all three shots taking effect. The colonel crashed dead from his charger, and a moment later guerrilla horses trampled on his body.

"Spread out — man to man!" shouted Grew, and blew a guerrilla's head off as the man swept past him.

The clash was ominous as the onsweeping guerrillas struck. Troopers were crashing dead from their horses under the point-blank revolver fire. A few turned to run, but were swiftly overtaken and dispatched by the killers.

Hand-to-hand duels began, as men picked their opponents and faced one another, shooting point-blank.

Experienced in battle, Lieutenant Grew, in the thick of it, knew that the dead colonel's error in tactics at the start of the battle, as well as the edge the guerrillas had in experience, had given his friends an insuperable handicap. Within minutes, the fight began to be a massacre!

There seemed no way that these maddened fighters of Quantrell's could be overcome. In no direction did it seem possible for the troops, being cut down, to look for sorely needed aid.

But at the Haven ranchhouse, the Rio Kid, having somewhat whittled down the odds against the sturdy Kansans, who were fighting beside him, had not failed to note the sudden withdrawal of Quantrell and the bulk of his guerrillas. A few had been left in the barn, holding the settlers in. Quantrell figured that the settlers would be glad enough for a lull, and would stay where they were.

"Boys, that must mean Grew and Terrell are comin'!" cried Bob Pryor, as he saw the killers gallop off northward. "I want twenty men to ride with me!"

"Why, we'll be slaughtered if we go out there!" shouted Milt Young. "Anyhow, our hosses are scattered on the plains, as yuh ordered, so Quantrell couldn't take 'em!"

"There's hosses at the barn, guerrilla hosses, and we're goin' to take 'em," Pryor said, his mouth grim and hard.

"I'm with yuh, Rio Kid!" Pop Schultz cried. "To the devil and back!"

"Me, too," Milt Young agreed then.

Every man in the house volunteered. The Rio Kid picked a score, choosing the youngest and best fighters, and led them to the back door of that house that was crowded with refugees — children and women, older men who must be protected. Pryor saw to it that his followers had plenty of Colt ammunition, and two guns apiece strapped on.

"See that side entry to the barn, boys?" he said. "Yuh're to go through it, and pronto. Give me just half a minute. I'm goin' to draw 'em to the other side. There ain't many left in there. Haven, cover me, will yuh?"

He pulled open the door, and dashed out, around the house. A bullet from a guerrilla in the barn whanged a chunk of mud from the corner of the house wall, but did not touch him.

The Rio Kid, shooting at the window of the barn, whenever he could see a guerrilla head, dashed full-tilt across the yard. Bullets kicked up mud and shrieked through the air about his head. Haven was shooting his rifle from a loophole, and the score of Kansans picked by the Rio Kid ran for the other side of the barn. They were halfway to it before the guerrillas, intent on the Rio Kid who was whistling as he ran, realized the game.

One defender went down, wounded, as Quantrell's men swung their guns on the moving settlers. But then they were at the barn door, and their pistols banged.

The dun with the black stripe down his

back appeared from the hill to the west, up over the raging creek, swollen by the rain. He came galloping to his master. The Rio Kid mounted bareback, twining his left hand in the dark mane, gripping with his knees. He had his right hand free for the Colt.

Shrieks of alarm rose in the barn, and massed gunshots roared. A couple of alarmed guerrillas appeared, squeezing through the opposite window, and the Rio Kid, galloping in, sent slugs into them.

The horses were the main objective, and Pryor dashed around to cover the animals of the guerrillas. Some thirty mustangs, saddled up and ready to go, stood with reins tied to the rail behind the barn.

He drove off several of Quantrell's devils who sought to escape, as Milt Young, leading the Kansans, raged through the barn and came out at the rear door.

"C'mon, boys — let them skunks go!" shouted Pryor.

Eight guerrillas, blasted from their horses, had taken to their heels and were running down toward the brakes along the stream, while half a dozen others, holed up in the stalls, prepared to stand.

Leaping on the mustangs, the trained cowboys and ranchers spurred forward and swung into line behind the moving Rio Kid. They galloped hard, in the direction Quantrell had taken.

Soon, topping a rise, the Rio Kid, fifty yards in advance of his score of fighting men, saw the battle raging ahead.

"On the flank, boys!" he shouted back. "Keep spread out and hold yore fire till you're on top of 'em."

The militia, cut down by a half in the first wild charge of the guerrillas, had their fighting blood up now and stubbornly contested the ground. Quantrell and his men were pouring lead into them but several guerrillas lay dead on the black plain which now was cut up into a slough. Horses slithered, and half fell, haunches coated with the sticky muck. Men's faces were spattered with it, and clothing was soaked and plastered.

The Rio Kid, his own fighting blood high in the exhilaration of the charge, and keeping low over his flying dun, hit Quantrell's flanks as the guerrillas made ready to charge again. Behind came his line of Kansans, Colts up and ready.

Holding fire till point-blank range was reached, the Rio Kid let go with his pistol. A guerrilla shrieked a curse and fell dead from his horse. And a few moments later the ranchers were in, their lead enfilading Quantrell's lines.

For the most part, the Kansans were deadshots, as good as the guerrillas, man for man. They aimed coolly and their slugs struck home, knocking vicious killers from their saddles. The enemy recoiled at the shock, then turned to face this new threat.

Seeing this, Lieutenant Martin Grew rallied his men with stentorian shouts, and charged.

Quantrell was in the thick of it, coolly directing his men. The Rio Kid rode at a mad gallop through the black muck of the cut-up plain, seeking to get around within revolver distance of Quantrell, and the huge Jarvis Thompson near the chief.

With the Rio Kid and his reinforcements in it now, Quantrell, a clever tactician, saw that the best he could hope for in the battle was a draw. The men he had meant to be victims had turned and were taking terrific toll of his men. A guerrilla scout — the Rio Kid recognized Jim Younger — spurred in from the east and spoke to Quantrell. A moment later, the guerrilla chieftain raised his hand, calling a retreat.

Balked by lines of guns that were continuously being fired, the Rio Kid took aim as Quantrell turned and rode off. He threw lead at Quantrell and saw the man's long-legged, powerful roan leap. Quantrell had to fight the roan, slamming a fist down between the beast's laid-back ears. Then the roan straightened out and went galloping southeast over the plain. The well-disciplined guerrillas moved off, after their murderous leader.

All the men left of the cavalry troop set up throaty cheers of victory. But they were too battered and their horses too worn out for them to attempt any long pursuit. The Rio Kid, with his score of Kansans, however, sought to harry the guerrillas, following them for a mile or two, but not enough men were with Bob Pryor to finish off the deadly horsemen.

For a time, this running fight went on, but the snarling Quantrell guns held off pursuit. Several men with the Rio Kid felt the sting of guerrilla lead before the chase was abandoned.

Moreover, the afternoon was drawing to a close, and the guerrillas were well-mounted and their horses rested from the day at the H Bar. Soon night would fall and Quantrell could, as he always did when hard-pressed, split his band up into small groups.

For once, though, the guerrilla chief could not claim a victory. Thirty percent of his men had been killed, and as many more wounded, mainly due to the strategy and the fighting prowess of the Rio Kid.

CHAPTER XIV
ON THE TRAIL

On the dun, Bob Pryor had ventured out ahead of his men in the chase after Quantrell's men. Jesse James and his brother, with half a dozen of the other guerrillas, essayed a quick, short charge, and forced him back. Quantrell, riding at the head of his band left that to them. His main purpose now was flight.

As the Kansans came up and the guerrillas drew off again, Pryor got down to study the fresh hoofmarks in the soft earth, left by Quantrell's roan.

"Huh!" he muttered, squatted by a clearcut hoof pattern. "I musta nicked that roan's forehoof!"

The left forehoof indention had a large bulge of mud inside it, meaning that a piece of it was missing. That explained why the roan had jumped as he had, after the Rio Kid's shot at Quantrell. This would have given the Rio Kid something of an advantage, and he was eager to go on. But his men were tired out, and the guerrillas on the run. Reluctantly the Rio Kid gave up the chase, after sending a final volley after the band, and swung back toward the H Bar.

The wounded were picked up and carried back to the ranch. The militia rode there also, to drink, rest and discuss the battle.

Just before nightfall, Captain Edward Terrell arrived at the Haven ranch, with two troops of trained but mud-spattered, worn-out cavalry, at his heels. The officer was infuriated at having been sent off on a wild-goose chase by the bogus Major Thompson, deeply regretful that he and his men had arrived too late to fight the guerrilla band. Terrell and his cavalry men had been riding for twenty hours without a break. The messenger sent after him by Lieutenant Grew had come up with him many miles east of Lawrence, and Terrell had turned and come back as swiftly as possible, but still too late to fight.

Sleep, food and rest were in order for everybody. The Rio Kid, still feeling the effects of his run up from Missouri with Quantrell on his trail needed more than anyone else to recuperate. So did his dun, for Saber had not yet recovered from the grueling journey.

Next day was warm and clear. The grass was sprouting up again through the muck, and soldiers and ranchers, refreshed, were out right after breakfast cleaning up their horses. The Rio Kid was among them, but his thoughts were not so much on helping remove the dried black mud that stained the legs of the animals after the battle north of the H Bar as they were on figuring how to overtake Quantrell.

Would the fox again break up his band to foil any organized pursuit, he wondered, and where would the chieftain himself head to, this time?

The Rio Kid consulted with Captain Terrell.

"If we could trail that roan — I can read his hoof sign like a printed page — we might track Quantrell himself," he suggested.

Terrell shrugged. "We'd better try anyway, I suppose. I'm determined to take that man, Captain Pryor. I've missed the devil a dozen times, but I'll never give up."

"That's the way to talk." Pryor grinned. "Let's brush up and get started."

Neither of those two young officers who had been sent by General U. S. Grant to take Quantrell would ever quit.

Leaving behind a few men who were too slow or too badly wounded to travel, Terrell still had over one hundred trained cavalrymen in Union blue behind him when he and the Rio Kid took up the guerrilla trail. Bob Pryor was in his element now. Expert scout and tracker, he could follow the now dried indentations of the three-score guerrillas who had retreated with Quantrell. For some miles it was as easy as reading a book, for the guerrillas had made no attempt to hide their tracks but kept on for the Missouri line.

The marks left by Quantrell's big roan horse held the Rio Kid's chief attention, however.

"I could follow that sign forever," he informed Terrell. "I nicked the animal's forehoof with a slug yesterday, and since I've seen the hoof marks left because of that I could never mistake them."

All day they stayed on the trail, now twelve hours old. The guerrillas finally had crossed into Missouri and reached the thickets they loved. The Rio Kid found that here they had split up into twos and threes, one of Quantrell's favorite tricks to hamper pursuit.

But even here the Rio Kid could count on the peculiar hoofmark of the roan to guide him. He picked it out from the maze of tracks that spread in every direction.

"Quantrell and three of his men have ridden due east," he told Terrell.

The cavalry troop camped in a woods for the night. But at the first streaks of dawn they picked up Quantrell's sign again and Bob Pryor stayed on it in spite of the attempts the guerrillas had made to hide it by riding through water and over stony sections of country.

Toward noon, pausing for water and a quick meal by a brook, the Rio Kid, after examining marks left by Quantrell and his handful in the soft earth by the bank of the stream, announced:

"That roan's gone lame, Cap'n Terrell!"

"Good!" cried Terrell, with fresh enthusiasm. "Then we may catch up with Quantrell at any time. Let's hurry."

"Wonder what he'll do?" mused the Rio Kid. "Try to find a new mount, I reckon, as soon as he can. He must know, by now, that his hoss is leavin' a plain trail."

Crossing the brook, the Rio Kid, out ahead of Terrell and his cavalry, picked up the guerrilla trail. Riding hard on it, in mid-afternoon he broke out onto a dirt road winding through the fresh green countryside of Missouri.

"East — east, always east," he muttered.

Quantrell had kept on in that same direction. Not once had he deviated from his course straight across the state.

Now Pryor found more signs left by Quantrell's roan. The animal was badly lamed now, and was getting worse. From the looks of the hoofprints Quantrell could not be so far ahead now, either. Then the Rio Kid saw a faint column of wood smoke rising over a low hill to his left, around a bend in the clay road.

"Mebbe that's where Quantrell is!" he thought. "If it is, Terrell will shore get him soon! That's him and his men comin' through the timber now!"

He had hardly caught sight of the troops, though, when his quick eye sighted something else toward the turn. He rode cautiously to it, and swore when he found it to be the body of the roan Quantrell had been riding. The once beautiful horse lay stretched in the ditch, a bullet through his head. He had been ridden to a frazzle, and was covered with mud collected from many sections of the country. But the mount had finally gone so lame that Quantrell had been compelled to shoot it.

Making sure that the guerrillas were not hidden close around this spot, the Rio Kid examined the forehoof of the dead horse. A big chunk had been shot from it, and the hole had caused a horseshoe nail holding the shoe on to loosen until the roan had stretched a tendon. Unable to get another mount in the woods, Quantrell had ridden the roan until he dropped, then shot him, either in mercy or fury.

Leaving the dead horse, the Rio Kid rode on, guiding his dun around. At once he saw the source of the wood smoke he had noticed. It came from the chimney of a farmhouse, a solitary home set, with its barn and outbuildings, in a green field. He reconnoitered carefully, but saw no signs that the guerrillas might be in there, though their trail turned into the lane.

Terrell was coming up, and signaling him. Knowing that the troops would follow, the Rio Kid galloped toward the farmhouse. As he rode around to the back he saw a girl standing in the open door. When she caught sight of him she quickly slammed the door, and he heard the bolt slide.

"Open the door, ma'am!" the Rio Kid called. "We're huntin' for fugitives from the law."

The girl appeared at the nearby window. She held a shotgun in her hands.

"Go 'way, you Yankees!" she screamed.

She had courage, though she was not more than seventeen. And the boy behind her, flourishing a big horse pistol was about twelve.

"We're after Quantrell, the guerrilla!" the Rio Kid called to the girl. "He passed here with three men not long ago. Don't shoot, sister. We won't harm yuh."

"Was that Quantrell?" she said, a sob choking her voice. "He killed Dad!"

She began to cry in earnest then, and flung open the door. The body of a Missouri farmer, a man of about fifty-five, with a graying beard and baldish head, was laid out on a bunk in the kitchen. The father of these two children, who were now orphans. For shortly the girl told the Rio Kid that their mother had died some years before.

The girl was afraid of the soldiers, but she talked freely to the Rio Kid. Her father, she said, had owned a splendid Arab, a black horse with a white patch on his right side. He had been exercising the animal, which he had managed to keep hidden from marauders up to this time, when Quantrell, riding double with one of his men, had suddenly appeared.

Quantrell had demanded the horse, offering Confederate money in payment. The farmer had refused, and in the argument, Quantrell had shot him dead, taken the horse, and ridden off with his men.

The Rio Kid cast about, hunting the new sign, hoping to follow Quantrell. After a time he came back.

"That Arab throws his right leg out when he runs, don't he, ma'am?" he asked the stricken girl.

"Yes, he does."

"Good. I'll be able to foller him, all right."

The Rio Kid gave the boy some silver money, and rode on.

As keen as a bloodhound that has picked up a hot, fresh scent, and aware that the laming of the roan had slowed Quantrell so that the guerrilla could not be many miles ahead, the Rio Kid shoved on, Terrell and his tiring troopers riding after him.

Close to sunset the Rio Kid, scouting ahead, reached a cross-roads. Here some twenty riders had met Quantrell but evidently they were friends, for the two parties had joined and ridden on eastward, toward the Mississippi River, which separated Missouri from Kentucky.

"Rendezvous," decided the Rio Kid.

He swung to report to Captain Terrell of the increase in the guerrilla force.

Terrell was ready to camp for the night. His troopers were tired from the long day in the saddle. Not much light remained. He listened carefully to Pryor's report.

162

"No doubt they arranged to meet here before they split up," he agreed. "We've got to stop for the night, now, though. Our horses are done in."

The elusive Quantrell, who had been not many miles ahead, had won another respite.

At dawn they took up the seemingly endless chase. By nightfall they had finished crossing the state of Missouri, and Quantrell's fresh trail still was hours old. The muddy Mississippi checked their progress. Quantrell had turned upriver, and crossed in the ferry at a little town about four P.M. The troops and the Rio Kid crossed in the same ferry.

They were in Kentucky, now, and Missouri was behind them. Quantrell was still in front, driving on with his fierce energy, but the men in Union blue pushed on after him relentlessly.

At noon, the following day, the Rio Kid rode up a dusty road to a small village — and got one of the most satisfying surprises of his life. He knew something unusual was up as soon as he saw the crowd of countrymen gathered about the porch of the general store and post-office. They were shouting and throwing their hats into the air.

"What's up?" inquired Pryor, dismounting to stretch his legs.

"Haven't yuh heard?" cried an old farmer, slapping him on the back. "Cap'n, yuh can shed that there uniform now! General Lee's surrendered!"

"Lee — surrendered?"

"Yes, *sir!*"

The stunning news made the Rio Kid's heart leap. Robert E. Lee, who had held off the Union's might during four years, who always had reserves, and always had managed to retreat and then counter-attack, had finally given up!

"Why, it means the end of the war!" shouted the Rio Kid.

For he knew that, without Virginia, the South could not hold out. The other Confederate forces must surrender.

He leaped on Saber and galloped back to tell Captain Edward Terrell the news.

"What!" shouted Terrell. "I can't believe it!"

He pumped the Rio Kid's hand, and, tearing off his hat, threw it into the air as he shouted the joyful tidings to his cavalrymen.

"Lee has surrendered — but Quantrell hasn't!" was the Rio Kid's grim thought.

He turned to the officer.

"I'll ride on, Terrell," he said.

CHAPTER XV
BIG GAME

During the afternoon, the Rio Kid passed another little settlement in Kentucky. The people there were excited, too, not only over the war, but because a detachment of what they believed to be Union soldiers had held up and robbed the town bank and the store, shooting and wounding two citizens in the process.

"Quantrell's up to his old tricks," thought the Rio Kid.

He explained that to the excited citizens. The guerrillas had put on Union blue and were riding in disguise, he told them, looting for food and cash as they moved. The Rio Kid figured they were heading for the wild mountains in the less settled sections of the Blue Grass State, hundreds of miles from Quantrell's usual stamping grounds.

Reaching the town of Taylorsville the following morning, the pursuers traveled along a well-beaten turnpike. It was difficult for the Rio Kid, now, with so many tracks, to distinguish the sign left by the black-and-white Arab which threw its foreleg, but his keen eye never faltered.

Now and then they passed a farmhouse set back, with its outbuildings, from the main road.

The day had started fair, but the wind had shifted and the sky was rapidly clouding up before mid-day had arrived. Soon rain began to fall, and Captain Terrell pulled his men off the road into the shelter of some big pines and prepared to wait out the storm.

But the Rio Kid was restless.

"I'm goin' to cast about some, Terrell," he told the officer.

"Why not let the storm blow over?"

"I figger Quantrell may do just that. I'll try a few miles further. Wait here, and then come down the pike slow, and I'll contact yuh."

"Very well." Terrell always took the Rio Kid's advice.

The rain was falling harder and harder, but the Rio Kid pressed on. He had a queer feeling that Quantrell might be very near, and his sixth sense usually guided him aright.

The storm was a fierce one. Thick purple

clouds broke open to throw buckets of water from the sky and the wind lashed and tore. The Rio Kid was soon drenched to the skin, despite all his clothing, while runnels of water flowed off the moving dun's flanks. During all the long, tiring chase the men who were relentlessly pursuing the murderous guerrillas had not encountered such a severe downpour.

The Rio Kid cursed as, with his head turned against the heavy southwest gale, he realized what this meant.

The dust and dirt were turning into liquid mud which, when it dried, would be smooth, and marks obliterated. Quantrell's tracks would be washed out and the guerrilla chief would once more elude him.

Suddenly he drew up. The guerrilla gang, some twenty-five horsemen, had swung off the road here! He could see the indentations of the hoofs leaving the pike. They had taken down the bars of a pasture, ridden through, then replaced the bars.

The pasture was on the same level as the road that ran through the great valley, but beyond, the slope rose to meet dark, dripping woods. As the Rio Kid stopped, turning his face into the wind, his sharp ears caught the unmistakable sound of several heavy reports, above the whistle of the storm.

"Revolvers!" he muttered.

He got down, removed the two wooden bars, rode across the field, and into the woods.

When he had ridden half a mile he could hear the shooting distinctly. Then the trees thinned out and in a brief lull in the blinding rain, he glimpsed a white homestead, with a big barn behind it.

Dismounting and creeping nearer, excited at the prospect of at last coming up with Quantrell, the Rio Kid saw some horses standing under a shed which ran around two sides of the barn. The horses were eating corn from racks — and one of them was a long-legged black with a white splotch on its side! The animal Quantrell had stolen from the farmer back in Missouri!

Heavy firing roared in the barn. The Rio Kid could not guess, for a time, what this meant. Then he decided that the guerrillas must simply be indulging in target practice, unaware they were so closely followed and believing the noise would be drowned out in the storm.

He hurried back to the dun and rode full-speed through the storm to the spot where he had left Terrell.

The rain pelted down with fiendish fury as the cavalrymen mounted at Terrell's quick commands. One hundred and twenty strong, Terrell's troopers slogged along the pike in the wake of the Rio Kid, swung through the pasture and up into the woods.

"Carbines ready, and loaded, men!" Terrell called.

They broke from the screen of woods, rushing for the big barn. The Rio Kid and Terrell were at the main gate; only fifty feet from the barn, when the firing inside suddenly ceased. A shrill cry reached their ears:

"Here they are! Here they are!"

Guerrillas came streaming from the door, to the shed, dashing for their horses. The Rio Kid was the first to open fire, then the troopers let go with their carbines. They leaped from their mounts and took shelter behind the fence circling the yard and barn.

Now a storm of carbine bullets tore into the twenty-five men about Quantrell. The Rio Kid recognized the guerrilla chief, in his Union blue uniform, a disguise Quantrell had so often assumed.

"Cut through, boys — don't surrender!" bellowed Quantrell.

Some of the guerrillas reached their saddles. It was every man for himself in such a case. Their revolvers snarled back at the

169

Federals, as Terrell sent men riding around to cut off their retreat.

Intent on Quantrell, the Rio Kid spurred along the fence, Colt ready in hand. But Quantrell, for once, did not have his usual luck. The Arab with the white splotch had jerked his head up and backed off as bullets spat close about him.

Quantrell was having trouble catching the mount. The guerrilla chief coolly walked into the hail of lead, seeking to entice the Arab to him with an ear of dried yellow corn. One of Quantrell's men, who had ridden away, glanced back and saw what trouble his chief was facing. At once he swung his horse and galloped to Quantrell, holding out a hand to help him up behind.

Quantrell sprang up on the horse, but the Rio Kid threw lead that way. The troopers also were sending in carbine slugs, and hardly had Quantrell mounted than the horse he was on went down. The man with the guerrilla chief threw up both hands and crashed dead at his leader's feet.

The Rio Kid and Terrell, with several Federals, were pushing in closer and closer to Quantrell — and he had no horse on which to escape! Many of his men, riding swift horses and splitting into groups, had dashed straight at the strung-out line of troops and had gone through to the woods beyond the barn.

Another guerrilla saw Quantrell's difficulty then. He turned back and offered his own horse to the chief.

But the Rio Kid and Terrell were close now, their eyes blazing with the excitement of the hunt. To them, Quantrell was a wild beast, murderous, deadly. He had cut his way out of such traps before and this time they were determined to finish him.

"Fire!" roared Terrell.

He threw up his Army Colt. The Rio Kid's was already blasting bullet after bullet at a range of fifty feet.

Carbines, too, were throwing their lead at Quantrell. The mount of the guerrilla who had come to save his cruel leader took slugs and crashed dead. The man leaped to the ground and began firing his revolver at the troops, but a moment later he staggered and fell.

Those guerrillas who had not died in the heavy volleys, had reached the thick woods, and were away. Only Quantrell of the whole band remained erect in the yard.

As the Rio Kid and the cavalrymen poured their fire at the guerrilla chief, with Quantrell's gun growling back, the guerrilla leader threw up both arms and flexed back, his bearded face twisting in agony. He was whipped around an instant later as by a giant hand, and his left hand flipped. He had been hit, again and again.

Then Quantrell, who had survived so many desperate situations, fell to the earth.

Dead guerrillas lay about their leader as the Rio Kid and Captain Terrell ran up, guns in hand.

Quantrell was still breathing, but he could not move his legs. Heavy rifle balls and pistol slugs had riddled him.

He looked up into the eyes of the men who had caught up to him, after so many years, this man with the blood of hundreds upon his head. He gritted his teeth but he did not cry out or groan.

"You're Quantrell, the guerrilla," Terrell said sternly. "You're my prisoner."

The Rio Kid squatted close by the terribly wounded leader. He knew a dying man when he saw one, and he knew that Quantrell had not long to live. He was ready to help the troopers when, at their captain's order, they picked up Quantrell and carried him over to the farmhouse.

Quantrell lingered, but it was obvious he could not pull through. Terrell had charge of the important captive, and the Rio Kid, his task finished, mounted the dun and left the place as the storm began to diminish.

CHAPTER XVI
DRYGULCHERS

After the big fight near the H Bar, Lieutenant Martin Grew felt that he must take time to recuperate from the wound dealt him by Jarvis Thompson, and from the strain of the battle. At George Haven's hearty invitation, he gladly agreed to stay at the ranch, where Edith could help care for him.

With the retreat of Quantrell, the defeat dealt the guerrillas, and with Terrell and the Rio Kid now chasing after the band, the settlers felt safe to return to their ranches. There were animals to be tended, and homes to be kept. Twenty-four hours after the departure of the troops, the H Bar had returned to normal. All the Havens' neighbors had gone back to their various spreads.

The weather was fine and once more men and women felt like going back to work with a will.

Haven did the work about his own ranch, with two cowboys helping him. Grew, relaxing near the girl he loved and whom he meant to make his wife, spent his time laying in the sun on a bench or strolling about the yard.

He had obtained money for Haven and for Haven's friends, so all of them now should be able to scrape through this lean season.

Grew kept expecting some word from the Rio Kid and Captain Terrell, but day after day passed with no news from the Union troops that were pursuing Quantrell. Then one day there was stunning news. A rider coming from town paused at the H Bar to give it.

"Lee has surrendered!"

Grew was delighted. He knew that meant the end of the long, awful Civil War. The whole range country knew that, and welcomed it, though the sympathies of so many of them were with the Confederacy.

Edith was a constant delight to Lieutenant Grew. Since she had promised to marry him he had never been so happy in his life.

But all of them were rudely shocked from their idyllic happiness and the new peace that had come on the land. It happened one morning, after breakfast, when Haven and his two cowhands left the house and crossed toward the horse corral, to saddle up.

Grew was indoors, helping Edith. Startled, they heard heavy guns roaring, and sharp yells from the three who had just gone outside. Snatching up his pistol, Grew ran over to the door and flung it open.

From the screen of brush along the creek he saw the smoke spurts of rifles. One of Haven's cowboys lay stretched in the dirt, while Haven himself was rolling over and over. The other H Bar man had made the barn and had turned, drawing a Colt.

"Mr. Haven, are you hurt?" cried Grew.

"Stay in there, Lieutenant — they'll get you!" shrieked Haven.

His face was contorted and Grew, seeing blood on his face was sure he had been badly hit.

The officer dashed out, crossed swiftly to Haven's side, and picked him up. A heavy bullet whirled past his head. But Haven was not so badly wounded that he could not run. He had only been dazed and bullet-scratched and he was shooting back at the drygulchers with Grew, when they reached the door.

"They killed Buck!" Haven growled, wiping the blood from the flesh gash in his cheek. "He crossed in front of me and I reckon they hit him 'stead of me. I ducked and one slashed me."

Bullets smacked the log walls and the door, but did no further damage. Then the H Bar cowboy in the barn began shooting down at the brush.

Grew peeked from a window, but he could see nothing in the screen of chaparral. Edith, hurrying to help her father, exclaimed in distress:

"Won't this fighting ever stop? I thought the war would be over."

A Colt began barking down by the river, and the carbines in the brush replied. Then Grew, watching, saw half a dozen riders flog from the woods and gallop off over the southern rise, on the other side of the creek.

A shout sent him to the other end of the building, and he recognized his friend, the Rio Kid. Pryor, a pistol in his hand, rode the dun into the yard, and unsaddled his weary mount.

"Cap'n Pryor!" cried Grew, hurrying to shake his friend's hand.

The Rio Kid was rested up from the long chase now. He had made a leisurely return to the H Bar, believing all danger had passed with the death of the guerrilla chief and the ending of the war. But he had arrived just in time to learn that danger was far from being over here.

"That was Jarvis Thompson shootin' over

there," the Rio Kid told Haven and Grew. "I reckernized the onery cuss as he dusted out of the brush. Some of his guerrilla cronies were with him. But we got Quantrell, Lieutenant — caught up with him in Kentucky."

"Thompson won't rest till he's killed me," growled Haven.

The Rio Kid nodded. He knew that Haven was right, but he meant to spike Thompson's plans. With Quantrell off his mind, he could concentrate on Thompson now, try to clear up the trouble of the Kansans, for which Thompson was chiefly responsible. It was Thompson who had set Quantrell on the settlers, and now he did not want to give up.

The Rio Kid drank deeply of the water Edith brought him.

"Thompson's shore hot on gettin' this range," he commented. "But he hasn't got Quantrell to help him now. Quantrell's bunch split up after the attack here, and the chief and twenty-five men headed for Kentucky. But there were others, and I guess still some of 'em throwed in with Thompson for this job."

"He must be mad," Grew said, "to keep after us this way."

The Rio Kid shrugged. "An hombre like

that," he remarked, "never does anything without a good reason for it. I'll have to look things over, and then we'll see."

The drygulchers did not return throughout the warm afternoon, but near supper time a messenger arrived from the Cross 4, one of the outlying ranches.

"Tim Bradley was shot and killed two hours ago," the rider reported, "by drygulchers!"

"Send out a warnin', Haven," the Rio Kid commanded. "In the mornin' I'll ride. . . ."

On the *qui vive* again, with the berserk, murderous Jarvis Thompson lurking with his killers in the brush and on the trails, the settlers were at a loss what to do. They dared not go about their work without keeping sentries posted, and any minute might bring a deadly rifle bullet sent from long range by the drygulchers.

The Rio Kid was eager to return to his command, to make his plans for the future. The ending of the war opened tremendous possibilities for all young men and he wanted to be up and doing.

He thought of his Texas home and of his parents, of how he could again return there. Possibly he might, in time, but right now other matters were claiming his attention.

Having rested Saber, the Rio Kid rode

from the H Bar the next morning, after cautioning Grew and Haven to be on guard against further attacks by Thompson. He had, thinking it all over, after the capture and mortal wounding of William Clarke Quantrell, a hunch which he intended to check on.

Not far from the Haven home, he came to the battlefield where by his flank attack, and with the aid of the settlers and the militia led by Martin Grew, he had smashed the terrible attack launched by Quantrell and Jarvis Thompson.

The sun had dried off the earth. He dismounted and examined the cut-up dark stuff.

Swinging into the saddle once more, he headed west along the creek, and after a time arrived at the Star 2, Milt Young's spread. Young greeted him cordially. He, too, was on guard, having received the warning sent out that Thompson was on the warpath.

That was the Rio Kid's first visit of the day, but he made many of them. His inspection of the ranches in the district occupied most of the day. He talked with the owners and looked over the range.

Thoughtfully, the Rio Kid returned to the H Bar, where Haven and Lieutenant Grew greeted him anxiously.

"What's yore plan?" Haven asked, watching the Rio Kid's keen face.

"I reckon we'll have to go after Jarvis Thompson," replied Bob Pryor. "He's set on wipin' yuh out, Haven — yore friends and you — and takin' over. He's outlaw now and figgers he might as well go whole hog or none. Yuh got any idea where Thompson and his killers might hole-up in these parts, handy, so's they could strike at the ranches when they wished?"

Haven shook his graying head.

"There are a good many streams in the neighborhood with timber along 'em," he observed, "and then there is broken country to the south where big rocks and groves and ravines split the plains. Might be in there, of course, but it'd be like huntin' a needle in a haystack if they wanted to lie low."

"One thing's shore," growled the Rio Kid, "and that is, Thompson won't quit. He'll lurk out there till yuh're off guard and then he'll strike again. If I savvied where his den was, we could go hit him right. How would yuh like to act as bait, Haven? Sooner or later Thompson'll try to drygulch yuh again and we might as well go to it."

George Haven shrugged, studying the Rio Kid's eyes.

"Anything you say goes, Rio Kid. Yuh've shore saved our bacon for us 'fore this. Hasn't he, Martin?"

Martin Grew heartily agreed. Had it not been for Captain Robert Pryor, the Rio Kid, he knew he would have been buzzard bait and so would most of the creek ranchers. They had thought that trouble all of the past, though, but here it was beginning again.

All over the range people prepared for trouble with outlaws, led now by Thompson who was coming to be as much feared as Quantrell himself ever was. At nights, the ranchhouses were dark, and the people who lived in them were ready for attack. Their doors were bolted and they slept on their guns.

Drygulchers must have light to see by, the Rio Kid was well aware, but in order to reach the ranchhouses they must do so in the darkness. Then they could lie up in the nearby thickets, watch for their victims, and shoot.

"Thompson wants to kill Haven more'n any of 'em," he decided. "I'll chance it."

Next morning, the Rio Kid gave the rancher instructions. Haven's cowboy guard was to be concealed inside the barn when on post, rather than where he might be spied on from the thickets. Pryor ostensibly took his leave of the H Bar, and rode away toward Lawrence as though on his way back East.

This was in case spying eyes might be on the place. Some miles away, well out of sight of the ranch, the Rio Kid cut south. Crossing the creek, he hid himself in the thickets, dozing away the warm afternoon.

As soon as dark came, he saddled the dun and rode slowly back upstream until he could see the narrow yellow-lighted windows of Haven's home. The folks were not asleep, and the candles glowed in the openings.

Unshipping his carbine and its belt of ammunition, the Rio Kid tethered the dun in the woods strip along the creek, hidden from view. He patted Saber, whispering to him to keep quiet. The well-trained animal understood, and would not neigh or break away.

Then Pryor laid a blanket near the stream bank, not far from the ranch, which lay across the river.

He slept, sure that the drygulchers would not try to strike until morning, at least. They should arrive, if at all, during the darkness, and to be safe from quick pursuit, the best time for them to open fire would be near sunset.

At dawn he was wide awake, chewing cold food, but he did not smoke, fearing to give away his position to the enemy should they be near.

The sun was warm and the day dragged interminably. Still the Rio Kid remained in his cover. He could see the H Bar buildings and the yard, across the creek, and George Haven moved openly about. Twice he saw Martin Grew, and Edith. But the cowboy was in the barn, out of sight.

Not a sign of the marauders disturbed the apparently peaceful countryside. Haven showed himself all day, acting as live bait. The rancher knew he was taking a big chance of catching a drygulcher's slug, but was willing to do so for the sake of his friends and neighbors, in the hope of trapping the killers.

As the sun reddened and grew bigger in the west, George Haven came out of the kitchen and walked slowly toward the barn. He did some work inside, then emerged, heading for the house.

The evening wind was freshening, and suddenly that breeze brought to the Rio Kid's ears the sharp crack of a rifle. Haven jumped and, putting down his head, ran full-tilt for the house.

There was another gun explosion. The Rio Kid, ready for just this, placed the shots as several hundred yards up the creek from his position. He hurriedly crept to the outer rim of the woods strip along the stream and watched. After a moment two horsemen rode full-tilt from the thickets, flogging and spurring their mustangs.

Chapter XVII
The Den

Neither one of the riders the Rio Kid saw was the huge Jarvis Thompson. They were clad in range clothing — Stetsons, leather chaps, high boots with silver spurs — and were heavily armed with pistols and rifles. The necessary belts of ammunition were draped over their shoulders and hanging from the horn of their saddles.

"Now or never," muttered the Rio Kid.

Stretched flat on his belly, he brought his steady Spencer to his shoulder. It was a long shot, at a swiftly moving object, and he aimed just ahead of the target as the leading drygulcher flogged up the shallow slope toward the rise, his partner galloping behind him.

The Rio Kid's rifle snapped with a cracking sound, the kick absorbed by his trained muscles. He watched with mounting excitement as the dark-hided mustang of the rider in the lead leaped and broke its stride. Then it picked up the pace again, dashing swiftly over the hill and out of sight.

"That did it!" he thought, "or I'm a farmer!"

Picking up Saber, the dun, who was restless from the long wait but had not made any whinnying complaint because of his careful training, the Rio Kid forded the creek and hurried to the H Bar.

"Halt — who's comin'?" a gruff voice called from the barn shadows.

"It's Cap'n Pryor. That you, Ole?"

"Yeah, yeah, Cap'n!" Haven's cowboy sentry cried. "Thought yuh was a drygulcher."

"What happened? Did they hit the boss?"

"Nope. Tore a hole in his shirt sleeve, though. It was mighty danged close."

The Rio Kid found Haven inside the house.

"Sooner or later they'll get me," the big rancher said matter-of-factly. "I heard that bullet comin', I do believe! It was only luck it missed my head, Cap'n."

"Yuh've done well, Haven," complimented the Rio Kid. "At dawn I'll be on the trail again. Yuh can take care of yoreself from now on."

Refreshed, and having eaten a warm breakfast, the Rio Kid crossed the creek and hunted for the trail he hoped would be there.

Sure enough, as he hit the brow of the hill, close to where the drygulcher had been the evening before when he had made his careful shot, he found a splotch of dark, dried stuff which he could easily pick out against the short grass of the plains.

It was blood, from the hide of the dark mustang forked by the assassin. The Rio Kid had figured that a crease under the animal's belly would produce such an effect; he had slightly wounded the horse and expected to be able to follow the sign.

For miles he could check the tracks of the pair who had sought Haven's life. Now and then he came upon a drop of blood, on a stone or a patch of grass, and was certain he was headed right. The killers had come riding southeast, toward the higher rocks and woods which George Haven had mentioned as a possible hiding-place.

The Rio Kid covered all metal from the sun. A flash would be a telltale in case the Thompson gang was watching for pursuit. Far ahead, he could see the rocks, and he did not wish to be observed heading for them.

Detouring from the blood trail, he found a drywash, one of the innumerable cracks that occurred all over the prairies. He rode along its stony bottom and so was down off the horizon of the plain. In this fashion he came to the broken section, in the afternoon.

He left the dun and, flitting from rock to rock and tree to tree, Indian fashion, cut over and at last located several tiny dark spots that he knew were blood drops from the slightly wounded mustang he was following. A faint animal trail wound below, into the recesses of the wooded, rocky hills, but he stayed up above, where he could see what went on and have more chance of escaping detection.

It was close to nightfall when the Rio Kid caught the faint odor of wood smoke. As dark fell he traced this slowly. It took him an hour to make a mile, but his patience was finally rewarded when he observed a faint glow in a tortuous, deep ravine.

Half an hour later, Pryor lay flat on a rock bluff, overhanging the outlaw camp, watching it.

The fire glow was faint, but he could see men lounging about on blankets. Many were smoking, and he decided there were ten or a dozen perhaps, in the little circle near the fire, which was carefully hidden by the bulge of the cliff face.

A cigar glowed ruby red at its tip — and the Rio Kid's keen eyes recognized the vicious face of Jarvis Thompson. Thompson had shed the Union uniform he had before worn, exchanging it for a leather jacket and riding pants, huge spurred boots, and a flat-topped Stetson. His skin was stained and dirty, and he was unshaven, but the Rio Kid knew him at once.

Pryor also sighted several other men he had seen before, guerrillas who had been at the rendezvous in Missouri. With Quantrell dead and the war over, they were joining up with Jarvis Thompson for further mischief.

"I tell yuh, we ain't got enough men, Thompson," the voice of one guerrilla rose to the Rio Kid. "There's twenty-five or thirty of them ranchers and they're on the watch now. Shorty and Dave missed Haven. The range was too long."

"That's right," growled Jarvis Thompson, his eyes glowing as fiercely red as the end of his cigar. "That's why I've sent for more of the boys. I got a message this afternoon that fifteen or twenty of the old band'll meet us here after dark tomorrer. Then we can go after them skunks shore enough, and clean 'em out of their dens."

"That's the stuff," another guerrilla agreed enthusiastically. "That's the guerrilla way."

Jarvis Thompson, thought the Rio Kid, was attempting to pick up where Quantrell, his partner, had left off. He was calling together Quantrell's guerrillas, for raiding.

"Once we've cleaned up here," he heard Thompson declare, "we'll head for Texas. They'll never catch us, boys. No use for any of yuh to try to go back to yore homes. Yuh're marked men. Yuh've rode with Quantrell."

Thompson yawned. "Let's turn in, boys. I'm plumb wore out."

Within a few minutes the raiders were rolled in their blankets, and beginning to snore, and the Rio Kid, retreating without a sound, hurried off to pick up the dun.

He had attained his first objective, to smell out the den of the killers.

The danger to his friends, the Kansans, was growing as Thompson, exposed as a criminal by the action of the Rio Kid, lashed out frantically in an effort to make a quick fortune and get away to other parts. The Civil War was over and there was no place in the civilized States that would offer such a man a safe hideaway. Thompson would be forced to use a front, but that would be easy. Once he had disposed of the ranchers he could help himself. . . .

At the crack of the next dawn, having

made the swift run back to the H Bar, the Rio Kid collected all the fighting men that the ranches could supply. Armed with carbines, shotguns, Colts and with ammunition for the weapons, the party numbered twenty-eight hard-bitten scrappers, grim, intent on vengeance and on wiping out the new threat to their safety and the lives of their loved ones.

With consummate skill, the Rio Kid brought his force as close as possible to Devil's Den, the patch of rocky, wooded country where Jarvis Thompson was lurking. There they awaited the coming of night, resting themselves.

As soon as dark fell over the land, the Rio Kid checked his men, making sure they were armed and ready. The horses were left in the deep drywash, with two older Kansans to hold them and keep them quiet, while the balance of the fighters followed the Rio Kid up into the ridges.

Knowing the site of the raiders' camp, Bob Pryor led his men straight to the height, then crept down to check up. The guerrillas were in their camp. They were awaiting the arrival of reinforcements, after which Thompson would strike.

The cookfire smoldered and the light down there was dim. The Rio Kid, aware that this would be the case, had prepared for it. He inched back, giving Haven signals with his hand, and the ranchers began crawling up into position on the bluff, guns ready.

Suddenly the Rio Kid's ear caught the sound of muffled hoofbeats, and the guerrillas in the den jumped up and went to greet the new arrivals. They were more of Quantrell's men, and they swelled Thompson's band to thirty hard-bitten gunfighters, making it about even with the Kansans. Pryor had hoped to strike before the reinforcements arrived, but it could not be helped.

He used the resultant noise and confusion to advantage. Getting to the edge of the rock bluff, he extracted a small flask from his inside pocket, one that he had carefully protected during the ride, and uncorked it.

He threw the liquid contents down on the smoldering red coals of the bandits' fire. At once a great flare of light came up. It was kerosene, which he had obtained from Haven's cask, which held the supply used in the lamps and lanterns.

The sudden rising light threw the raiders into easy relief for the men above.

Stunned by the unexpected glare, they froze in their tracks, staring at the fire, unable to guess what had occurred.

The Rio Kid's stentorian shout rang through the den:

"Throw down, outlaws! You're covered!"

Chapter XVIII
Fortune

Jarvis Thompson was the first of the outlaws to recover his wits. The big chief was to the Rio Kid's left, greeting the horsemen who had just come in. As the fire flared up, he dropped his hair-flecked hand to his Colt, whipped it out.

"Fight, you fools, fight!" he roared.

The Rio Kid's thumb rose from his Colt hammer. The oil was still blazing high, but it would be only a minute or so until it would burn away.

Thompson was hit. Staggering back, he fell to one knee by a large rock. Then his pistol snarled back, and the Rio Kid felt the whirl of lead close by his cheek.

"Let go, boys!" Pryor yelled to his men.

The guerrillas were drawing, aiming up at the dark shapes of the ranchers on the bluff.

A scattered volley rang out, but the Kansans, taking careful bead on individuals, steadily replied. Six outlaws took bullets, and fell out of the scrap. The riders sought to swing their mustangs and fight out to the trail, but the Rio Kid's men whipped deadly carbine bullets into them. Their horses bucked and reared in panic. Raiders were running about, hunting cover from which to fight, while shotguns spread their tearing buckshot over the gathering below.

The Rio Kid was concentrating on Jarvis Thompson. Feeling the accuracy of Pryor's lead, the big man jumped up and dashed, zigzagging, across to the other side, where he plunged into the brushy rocks. But on the way, he was ripped by a second slug from Pryor's swift Colt.

"I want him more'n any of 'em," muttered the Rio Kid. To Haven he called, "Take over, Haven!"

The smashed, bleeding guerrillas, half of them crippled, milled in the confines of their den. The exit was blocked by plunging mustangs.

The Rio Kid ran up the rim, and went sliding down into the cauldron. He dashed across, and came down in the shadows toward the spot where Jarvis Thompson had holed up.

"Thompson!" he roared, over the battle din. "Come out with yore hands up!"

A Colt barked at him from the rocks. He

threw slugs that way, and ran in.

A moment later he glimpsed a Stetson as Thompson rose up to kill. He had an impression of a snarling, gritted teeth, face, and was half-blinded by the flare of Thompson's revolver. But he had already started his own slug on its way, aimed at the furious, bearded features of his arch-foe.

Something cut a chunk from his boot side and plugged into the earth. But Thompson's gun had not risen far enough before the Rio Kid's finishing bullet had struck home.

In the dying light, the Rio Kid saw the big fellow lying limp over his rock top, arm stretched out. He moved in, aware that the shooting was dribbling off.

Jarvis Thompson was dead, drilled through the head. The Rio Kid's bullet had smashed his nose and cut up to kill instantly.

Turning, with his Colt ready, Bob Pryor threw a couple of bullets into a patch of guerrillas who were still stubbornly fighting. Others had tossed down their guns and lain flat to keep from being annihilated. A few, mounted and near the exit, had escaped.

Haven and his friends came sliding down to take their prisoners. Thompson was smashed, the Kansans were safe. And the Rio Kid gloried in that. . . .

A little later, the settlers had gathered at

Haven's H Bar, to celebrate the stunning victory over their enemies. Bob Pryor, the Rio Kid, was telling them of the lure which had driven Jarvis Thompson to the horrible lengths he had undertaken.

"And that's what Thompson was after gents," he reported.

"Coal!" exclaimed Haven. "By glory, I never guessed it!"

"There are vast beds under yore range," the Rio Kid insisted, "far as I've been able to make out. That black muck north of here started me thinkin', and I noted some sheeny specks on the horses when it had dried. Thompson was plumb excited over somethin', and I checked up. Coal's worth millions in big quantities and yuh've got that in these parts. Yuh kin sell off some of yore land, and clean up fortunes. No need to worry over anything from now on."

"I thought it was the range he was after, to sell for land!" said Milt Young.

"Me, too," nodded Pryor. "That's what Thompson told Quantrell, when I overheard 'em at their camp. But Thompson didn't even let Quantrell in on the real secret. I reckon he hoped to cheat Quantrell in the end and keep the money for hisself. After Thompson was exposed, of course, that meant he would have to pay somebody to act as a front for him, but that would be easy enough. Then, when he had sold the coal deposits for a big sum, he would run for Texas and live at ease on what he had."

The Rio Kid's discovery had electrified the Kansans. From abject poverty, wondering how they would manage to skin through another year and hold on to the devastated ranches, they were wealthy.

Haven and his friends begged the Rio Kid to remain with them, but Pryor was eager to be on his way back to his command.

He took his leave the following morning. The dun was groomed and sleek, and the Rio Kid was wearing his uniform of a Union officer.

Martin Grew, with Edith Haven clinging to his strong young arm, smiled good-by to his friend, the Rio Kid. Haven looked regretful, at losing Pryor, but duty called.

He waved his hand, and started away. The debonair Rio Kid was on his run back to the Potomac, his mission successfully accomplished. And behind him, the Rio Kid left contented, joyous friends. Martin Grew was engaged to Edith, and their fortunes were made for the life they would have together, forgetting the horrors of Civil War.

Around noon, Pryor reached Lawrence. Burned shells of houses still attested to the terror of Quantrell's horrible raid.

He dismounted in the center of the town, to eat, and to rest Saber.

Crowds of excited citizens milled in the streets. Shouts, curses, wails filled the air.

"What's up, pardner?" the Rio Kid inquired of a man who was weeping, tears flowing unashamedly from his eyes.

"President Lincoln has been assassinated!" the man gasped.

"Lincoln!"

The Rio Kid felt part of his soul die. He knew Lincoln, the great War President, and had looked to him as the Nation's hope, both for the victorious North and the bleeding, battered South.

Dazed, he shook his head. Lincoln, dead!

There was no stability in the world. It changed continually, and it moved madly, swiftly, in its modern pace.

Then he caught hold of himself. Slowly he went to Saber, touched the animal's sleek neck. The dun nuzzled lovingly at his hand.

The Rio Kid mounted and rode away. The wild trails called him and he would answer.

We hope you have enjoyed this Large Print book. Other Thorndike, Wheeler, and Chivers Press Large Print books are available at your library or directly from the publishers.

For information about current and upcoming titles, please call or write, without obligation, to:

Publisher
Thorndike Press
295 Kennedy Memorial Drive
Waterville, ME 04901
Tel. (800) 223-1244

or visit our Web site at:

http://gale.cengage.com/thorndike

OR

Chivers Large Print
published by BBC Audiobooks Ltd
St James House, The Square
Lower Bristol Road
Bath BA2 3SB
England
Tel. +44(0) 800 136919
email: bbcaudiobooks@bbc.co.uk
www.bbcaudiobooks.co.uk

All our Large Print titles are designed for easy reading, and all our books are made to last.